the

secret

language

of

spiders

# praise for
# the secret language of spiders

*"An assured and unsettling debut novel. If you love King, you're going to want to book a trip to Kobbe's End. Can't wait to see more from K.L. Young."*
-Mark Rahner,
(Rotten, Vampirella, The Twilight Zone)

*"K.L. Young's debut novel masterfully spins a terrifying tale of love, death, and the lies we weave to keep from accepting the inevitable truth... and the horrific consequences."*
-Pete Rawlik
author of Reanimators and
The Weird Company

*"In my youth, I attended summer camp outside of a small, rural town named Kobbe's End... much against my will. It was here, in my nerdy innocence, that I was first bullied by The Secret Language of Spiders. Pushed around by its grotesque descriptions, taunted in my bunk at night by its whispers of unseemly eight-legged horrors thick as moss on the forest floor, teased mercilessly by its lyrical prose in the showers while everyone laughed. I was told this would build my character by adults. They were right."*
-Seth M Sherwood.
screenwriter of Leatherface and
HellFest, former small-town tragedy case.

Also written by K.L. Young

<u>chapbooks</u>

*The Ballad of Erik Zann*
*(Illustrated by Rob Corless)*

*Infernal Combustion*
*(Illustrated by Ben '1314' Hansen)*

*Shaine The Hellslinger*
*(Illustrated by Rob Corless)*

<u>novellas</u>

*Widowed*

<u>screenplays</u>

*Sunset*
*Widowed*
*Thorns*
*Kosek*
*Killer's Moon*
*december*

available at
www.writtenbyklyoung.com

STRANGE AEONS

© 2024 K.L. Young
Cover art & design © 2024 Faquahd Graphics

This book is a work of fiction. Names, characters, places and incidents are either a product of the author's imagination, or used fictitiously and any resemblance to persons living, dead, or metamorphosing into a gigantic spider is purely coincidental.

All rights reserved. No part of this publication may be reproduced in a retrieval system, or transmitted in any form or by any means electronic, mechanical, photocopying, recording or otherwise without prior written permission from the publisher.

This book was previously published in a very limited signed and numbered edition.

Strange Aeons LLC
Seattle, WA
USA

www.strangeaeons.net

the secret language of spiders

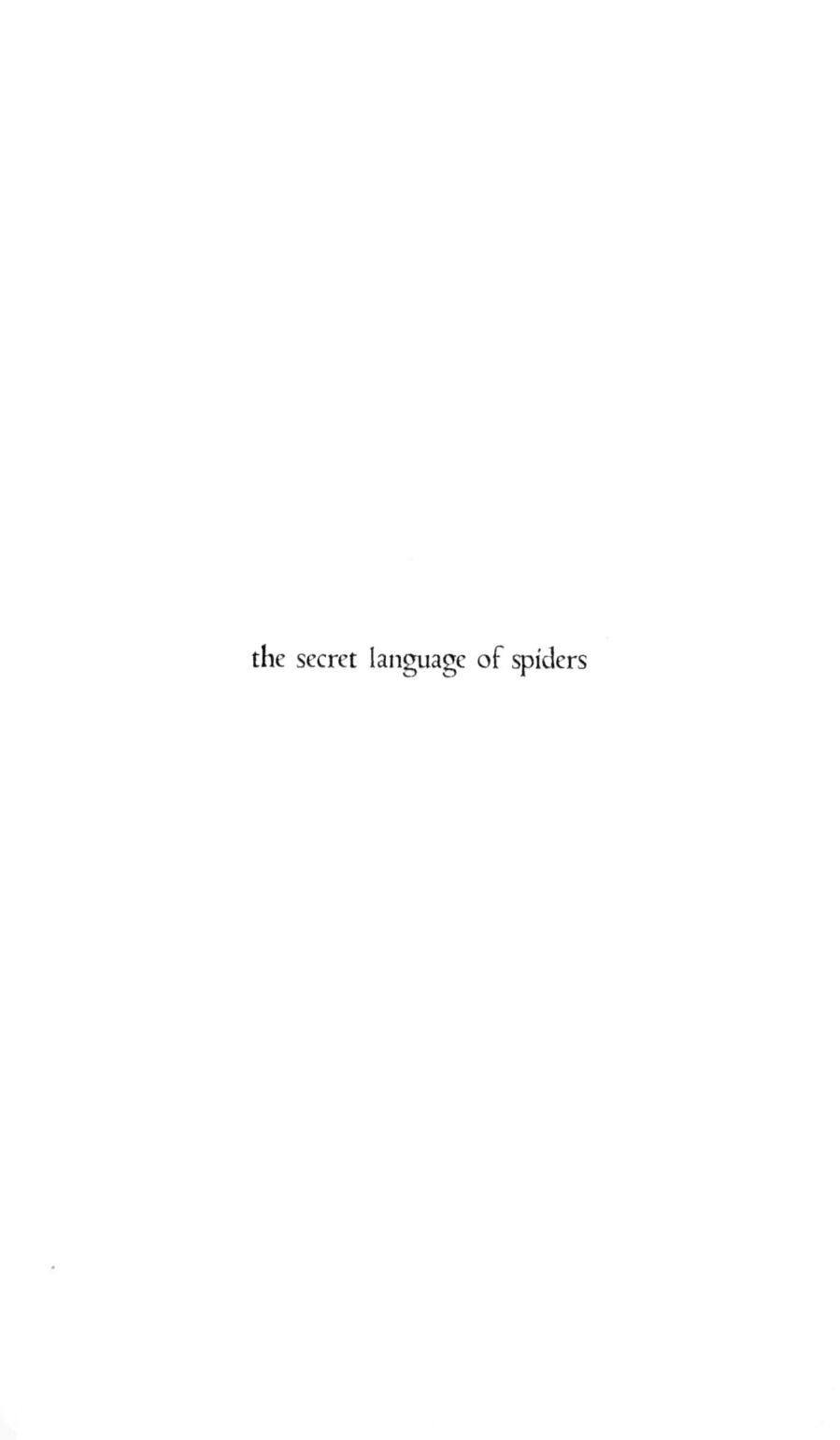

*TLOML*

# part one:

# a smile at midnight

# I

On the morning of the eighteenth of September, 1884, the three hundred sixty-three souls that called home the tiny town of Kobbe's End woke to what appeared to be a fine layer of snow covering everything, sparkling in the sunrise of what promised to be a record day of heat.

It was not snow, however, that blanketed the roads and the trees and the roofs of the eight buildings (some little more than glorified tents) that framed Main Street, but an astonishing amount of spider webbing, blown across the plains and carrying thousands upon thousands of spiders to their new home.

The still waters of Tillman's Depths on the outskirts of town seemed to snag a majority of the webbing, looking as if it had frozen solid in the heat, the silky strands so thick upon the lake that the spiders would have been able to crawl without issue to the shore, had that been their destination.

Spider migrations are common near the end of summer, but the sheer magnitude of this one made the record books, and the founders of the town, Decraine Kobbe and Richard Tillman, saw it as a sign of prosperity, and to this day - one-hundred-and-forty-some years later - the event is celebrated still with a festival full of fake webbing and rubber spiders, signaling the beginning of fall for the somewhat larger (but still tiny) town, whose residents number near the eight thousand mark, today.

One of those residents was Daniel Cook, who was making his way home through fresh snow this winter morning, gloved and booted, carrying two paper bags filled with groceries from Williford's Supermarket, and wishing he had just taken the K-Car they had been gifted by a parishioner who had fled the dying town earlier that year.

The Wal-Mart between Kobbe's End and the next town, Sunset, had closed their doors a few months back because of rising criminal activity, and Daniel was grateful that Williford's had somehow weathered the COVID closures. Not only because he liked the family that ran the supermarket, but because it was within reasonable walking distance, and although the roads were mostly clear, he didn't trust the tread on the old Chrysler's tires.

He made his way past berms of brown-black snow plowed against the facades of boarded up businesses, abandoned cars, and the homeless encampment that had sprung up in the long-vacant lot next to Morgret & Sons hardware.

Kobbe's End had certainly seen better days, most notably in the '90s, when mercury and copper mining made the town very desirable, but the mines had dried up a few years back, and the pandemic and closures sure hadn't done them any favors, and the 'End, as it was colloquially known, appeared to be a terminal patient on failing life support.

Daniel hardly noticed, long past caring about the decay and ruin that surrounded him as he trudged home. He had more important matters on his mind.

"Nancy," he called out from the kitchen, after removing his coat and hat and kicking his wet boots off at the door. There was no answer, and he started transferring groceries from the sacks to the cupboards. "Would you like some tea?"

Still no answer, and he hadn't really expected one, but there was an ominous and now-familiar whisper at the back of his brain that said, *It happened today. She's finally gone.* He pushed the thought away and put the kettle on the stove.

He nudged open the upstairs bedroom door with one foot. Nancy lay still in the bed, frail and sick, and that terrifying whisper in his brain started up again, but she turned her face and smiled warmly at him as he sat in the chair next to her, offering a mug of hot tea.

"*Tieguanyin*," he said, as she struggled to sit up in the bed, taking the mug from him. "For my iron goddess."

"Oh, hush," she said, but she smiled at their old joke, and Daniel couldn't help but notice the lines around her eyes, around the corners of her mouth. Daniel was pushing fifty-five, and she ten years younger, but today you might be forgiven for mistaking her for his mother.

The last year had been devastating, starting with a spider bite on her shoulder that had turned into a nasty infection and set off a string of mystery ailments that baffled six doctors and the entirety of the internet. Angry and afraid and no longer willing to be studied, Nancy had made her wishes known: If she were going to die from this - and that certainly seemed to be the case - she wanted to do it in the comfort of her own home.

"You're going to be late," she said, sipping at the steaming mug.

"They can wait," Daniel said. "Careful, it's hot."

"Feels good," she replied, taking a bigger gulp.

"How is it today?"

She knew he didn't mean the tea. "Not so bad," she lied. "Better than yesterday."

Yesterday had been the winner in a series of escalating pain days, and Daniel didn't like the mottling that had sprung up seemingly overnight in the skin around her temples. But he smiled and brushed a strand of dull, graying hair away from her eyes. "Good. You'll be up and causing trouble again in no time."

Neither of them believed that, but Nancy smiled at him and for a moment, he could see the beautiful woman he had met twenty-five years earlier. "If it's God's will, I'll make it through this."

"Hmph. God." Daniel scowled. "If we have to rely on that son of a bitch, we're in a world of trouble."

"Shh, Danny. You need to go to work."

So he put on his gray suit and his silver cross and went down to deliver his sermon.

# 2

The church that was connected to their townhouse was small, old, and like the rest of Kobbe's End, slowly disintegrating. The maroon carpet that ran down the single aisle was worn thin, the weathered oak pews in need of a fresh coat of varnish.

Behind Daniel's lectern and off to the side was a relic of the church's recent past, a nine-foot-tall abstract art sculpture of a cross from when the church had made a disastrous attempt to connect with a younger congregation in the early 1990s. The cross, constructed of two rusting

I-beams and welded messily together at the juncture, twisted maniacally from the floor it was bolted to.

When Daniel took over duties as the regular pastor only a few years later, they quickly discovered that the art installation weighed well over four hundred pounds, and simply unbolting it from its base on the stage would be a major process. And so there it loomed, certain to make uncomfortable any child unlucky enough to have been dragged into this house of worship. Not that the church had seen a child walk through its doors in the last decade or more.

His congregation numbered less than a dozen today and were also aged and worn through in spots. Most of them were ten or more years older than him, although some still held a spark of life, or a reasonable facsimile.

As was his custom for the last several months' worth of Sundays, he lied to them for nearly an hour.

He said things like, "We know there is evil in the world. We can turn on the computer and see an uninterrupted stream of it every day. But why is there so much? Why would a loving God allow this to happen?"

He said things like, "As the heavens are higher than the earth, so are His ways higher than our ways, and His thoughts higher than ours."

And he said things like, "Your children don't always understand the reasons behind what you allow or do not allow them to do. Why should we expect to understand all of God's reasons for allowing all that He does?"

But none of it rang true to him anymore, and by the end of the sermon, he thought when Nancy finally caught the last train out, he would most likely take his own life rather than continue to exist in a world without the woman he loved.

The chilly, dismal sky over Serene Hope Church loomed darkly, threatening more snow as the smattering of humanity left the building, filing past Daniel and the little plastic reader board that exclaimed, "WHY DOES GOD ALLOW EVIL?", and under that, "Pastor Daniel Cook."

Daniel smiled and nodded at each body that shuffled past: at Ellie Lang, who could barely remember her own name most days; at Beatriz Rodriguez, who tipped the scales at well over three hundred pounds; at Rick Lai, who had owned the only theater in town before COVID killed his business; and at Jenny Thomas, bringing up the end of the short line and wearing a hat that would have turned heads at the Kentucky Derby.

She stopped and grinned, her eyes nearly disappearing behind her ruddy cheeks. "An excellent sermon today, Daniel."

"Thank you, Jenny," he said, trying to tear his eyes away from the swooping brim and gargantuan faux flowers atop her head. "That's some hat."

She beamed. "I very much enjoyed the analogy of us being children who cannot understand God's rules."

Daniel nodded and smiled graciously. He didn't have the heart to tell her he'd found the sermon online.

"It's such a shame you and Nancy had no children - you would have made wonderful parents."

Daniel's thoughts flashed briefly to the two miscarriages Nancy had endured before they both decided that children were not meant for them. The second was over fifteen years ago, and if asked to chart the journey of his loss of faith, it must surely have begun then. "We always wanted, but it just never happened for us."

She gave a sympathetic cluck, and this time, Daniel's smile was genuine. Over the last few years, an easy and natural friendship had sprung up between Mrs. Thomas and the Cooks. They were all a little too old for new friends, and the 'End was tough ground for relationships to take root, but the three of them shared lunch, paperbacks, and baked goods semi-regularly, and Jenny would routinely fill Nancy in on her favorite new true crime documentaries on Netflix. She was one of the good ones, sticking around as the congregation continued to dwindle. It would have horrified her to learn of his thoughts at the lectern during the service.

"How is Nancy? Feeling better, I hope?"

"About the same, unfortunately. Thanks for asking."

"I'd like to come by sometime this week, if I might. Just to say hello."

"Well, I'll let her know, but she really hasn't been feeling up to visitors lately."

"Sure, sure," Jenny nodded, not quite ready to give up. "Some of my famous yeast rolls, maybe? I'll swing some by and see if she's up for a visit."

"That would be nice," Daniel said, and he meant it.

As the woman made her way down the church steps, faded from countless cycles of freeze and thaw, Daniel noted an older man in a crisp gray suit, waiting for her to pass so that he may head up.

His shock of white hair gave him away, and when the man reached the top step, Daniel smiled and shook the proffered hand with genuine affection.

"Michael," he said warmly, "What brings you to fabulous Kobbe's End?"

Michael Davis jerked a thumb in the direction of the homeless encampment down the road and chuckled. "It certainly isn't making any top-ten travel destination lists, is it?"

"In our defense, you're visiting during our brutally cold Winter season. You should really come back for our unbearably hot Summer. That's when the drug dealers come out of hibernation. Nature is amazing."

Michael smiled. "It's nice to see you, Daniel. I'm sorry I missed the sermon. How was it?"

"Oh, you know. A lot of 'God is good, God is great' kind of stuff. Nothing you don't already know. Join me for a cup of coffee? Tea? Fentanyl?"

"Tea would be great," Michael said, grinning. "Hold the fentanyl."

After motioning him inside and locking the church doors, Daniel led Michael toward the last row of pews, fishing in his pocket for the key that fit the privacy lock in the handle of the door that connected their townhouse to the small church hall.

Michael grimaced as they passed the giant abstract cross. "You still have this thing up?"

"Came with the church," Daniel replied, unlocking the door's simple privacy lock. "It's too heavy to move by myself, and even if I could, what would I do with it? Besides, I think it actually comforts some people."

"You can't be serious."

"Sure," Daniel said, leering at the cross. "Who wouldn't want to see their savior crucified on this lovely piece of art? Industrial Jesus welcomes you!"

The two of them sat at the kitchen table with the checkered tablecloth, tea bags steeping in their mismatched mugs. Daniel smiled politely, watching Michael silently judge the quaint and outdated décor of the kitchen. He found himself getting annoyed with his old friend, who lived in a lovely, church-owned home in neighboring Heather.

"Sure I can't put something in your drink?" Daniel finally offered.

"Oh, no, no," Michael said. "Not today." He took a sip from his mug, then used his spoon to stir it a bit more. "How's Nancy doing?"

Daniel weighed his words. "Not well."

Michael sighed deeply, focusing on his tea. "Ah, hell. I'm sorry. Still no idea what we're facing?"

Daniel choked down his annoyance at the use of the word *we're*. "The Lord works in mysterious ways," he replied, feeling immediately guilty at the sour look that Michael shot him. "Sorry. The doctors still think it's cellular degeneration caused by necrosis around the spider bite. Or something…

we don't even know anymore. It's out of control now. The meds are no help."

"Do you know Peter Rawlik?"

The name didn't sound familiar. "No. Should I?"

Michael shrugged. "He's a very smart doctor, a specialist. And Christian. He's taken an interest in Nancy's case, and-"

"No. No more doctors. She refuses. And I just won't put her through it anymore. She spent almost eight months being poked and prodded in there, and in the end, all those specialists shrugged their shoulders and gave up on her."

They sat in uncomfortable silence for a few moments. Finally: "Keep the faith, Daniel. God will- "

Daniel slammed his hand on the table hard enough to rattle their spoons. "Oh, fuck God," he hissed.

Michael frowned, pained. He reached across the table and took Daniel's hand, squeezing it tightly. "Do you have anyone to talk to? You don't have to face this alone, you know. You have friends. I'd be happy to -"

Daniel waved him off before the older man could finish. "No, no. I'm sorry. I shouldn't have said that."

"I understand your frustration. If you don't want to talk to me, you know the church can provide a counselor."

Daniel felt a wave of shame roll over him for blaspheming in front of his oldest friend in the church, the man that had married him and Nancy twenty-one years earlier. He could feel tears threatening behind his eyes.

He stood up abruptly, straightening his tie, ending the visit. "Thanks for stopping by, Mike. I've got a busy day ahead of me, so…"

But Michael stayed seated, his eyes focused on the mug he cradled in both hands. "There's something else."

*A-ha,* Daniel thought. *The other shoe.*

"The church is crunching the numbers," Michael said slowly, and Daniel knew exactly where he was going. "The numbers here in the 'End. They're just too low to justify keeping the church open."

Daniel nodded, trying to keep the relief he was feeling from flooding over his face. He had carried the fear of an impending closure due to numbers - numbers preceded by dollar signs – around his neck for the last eight years as the population of the tiny town dropped lower and lower, and this news should have crushed him. Instead, he felt a massive weight lifted from his chest.

"I understand completely," he said. "How much time do I have?"

Michael met his eyes, surprised at first, but pushing quickly past it. "Sixty days. I'm sure when you're ready you can request a relocation. You know. When you're..." he struggled to find a word, finally settled on, "...ready."

Daniel smiled at his old friend. "You know, I don't think I'll be doing that. I've actually been thinking of... retiring."

*the secret language of spiders*

# 3

 Wade Chitwood sat in his '98 Ford Bronco with the faded Kobbe County Sheriff badging on the sides, studying the parking lot of the Kwik-E mart across the way from the closed-down Chinese restaurant he was parked next to.

 He rubbed at his forehead just between his eyes, feeling the slight pressure of a headache brewing. They were coming more and more often these days. He didn't like to think about it.

 When he was a teen in the 80's, he and his buddy Ben had spent many a Friday evening after school hanging out in that parking lot, blasting Dokken or the 'Scorps out of the blown-out speakers in his Chevy Monza, hitting on girls and bumming smokes off passersby.

 A lot of shady stuff had gone down in that parking lot back then, fights over girlfriends, underage drinking, even the occasional drug transaction. Light stuff, mostly weed and very rarely coke, nothing like what the kids were doing these days.

In fact, some kind of deal was going down in the lot right now, and he squinted to see what was trading hands in the crisp and cold shade of the Kwik-E Mart sign.

*Not weapons,* he thought, grateful. *Definitely just drugs. But just as deadly, anymore.*

Even the coke these days was laced with something, often just filler chemicals, boric acid, or levamisole, but sometimes something much, much worse.

He waited for money to change hands, then turned the old Bronco's roof bubble on, chuckling at the surprised looks on the faces of the two men as he pulled into the parking lot.

He recognized both the seller - Rahner, a common hood from Sunset that Chitwood had busted at least a half dozen times over the last few years; and the buyer, the DaBronzo kid,

*Nikos, I think his name is*

just eighteen and an on-again-off-again member of the growing homeless community in the big vacant lot by Morgret & Sons.

Chitwood didn't much care about the kid. He was just another deadbeat symptom of the rot and ruin that had hit Kobbe's End since the mines had closed.

But Rahner was part of the disease, and the sheriff had become increasingly tired of watching his town fall apart all around him.

Chitwood had lived in Kobbe's End for forty-nine of his fifty-five years, and he'd just celebrated three decades in the Unincorporated Kobbe County Sheriff's Office. For the last ten years he'd been the acting sheriff, but he knew that was mostly due to running unopposed after Sheriff Mullin had been discovered sleeping with a high school student and embezzling Office funds.

No one wanted the job, including Chitwood, if he were being honest, but he wasn't going to sit idly by and watch his hometown flounder while the state twiddled their thumbs and tried to figure out what to do with the situation.

Since then, he'd busted two meth labs and a considerable gambling ring connected to the local Indian casino, both of which plunged the town into a deepening depression and decline.

The Sheriff's office had shrunk to eight employees because of his diligence, which meant today he was actually on patrol, driving the old Bronco through the falling snow and slushy county roads, his tongue repeatedly poking and digging at the empty slot of a front tooth that had yet to be repaired and probably never would be. He wasn't exactly worried about impressing anyone these days. Besides, he'd grown his mustache so thick that it nearly covered his entire mouth, and he'd gotten perversely used to prodding at the empty space where the tooth had been.

As the Bronco jumped the curb, both Nikos and Rahner scattered, the teen racing down the snowy back alley behind the Kwik-E Mart.

Chitwood knew he'd never catch the kid, even if he wanted. The alley was unplowed, and the Bronco wouldn't handle the twelve inches of frozen snow easily.

He also knew he could find Nikos in the vacant lot full of tents or, barring that, at the house the kid's mom lived in, where he'd let the old ball-buster know her son was in trouble again.

But he knew he wouldn't do that. The paperwork on this kind of nothing-burger arrest just wasn't worth the collar. He'd let the kid skate this time. Today he had bigger fish to fry.

And so Nikos DaBronzo escaped into the dim afternoon, headlong into a series of events that would soon lead to a very grisly end for the troubled boy.

When Nikos fled, he'd dropped the little baggie of smack he'd been holding, either panicking or smart enough to know he didn't want to be caught with it.

But Rahner had turned the other way, gripping his cash payment and rushing to the late model X-5 that was idling nearby.

*Should've done the deal in the car,* Chitwood thought, but knew Rahner would never let a scumbag like Nikos into his vehicle.

Chitwood didn't like his odds of keeping up with - much less catching - the German SUV in the snow. He made an executive decision, spinning the Bronco's steering wheel deftly between his cracked and calloused hands, aiming to slide right next to the Bimmer's driver door and block Rahner from entering.

Instead, the Bronco's tires spun on the compacted snow of the Kwik-E Mart's lot, and he could only watch with a groan as his vehicle's front bumper clipped Rahner at the hip, body-checking the dealer into the air - just a couple feet - and sending him face-first into the frozen snow.

The Bronco finally slid to a stop, and Chitwood stepped out, hand on the butt of his holstered .45.

"All right," he said, crunching through the snow and gripping Rahner's shoulder to turn him over. "You're all right, come on."

He was relieved to see that Rahner *was* mostly all right, his face red and wet from his impact with the snow, but he seemed to stand fine, and Chitwood sighed with relief. The last thing he needed was some kind of excessive force investigation.

"Against the vehicle," he said gruffly. "Hands on the hood."

"I know," Rahner said, irritated. "I know, I know."

Chitwood pushed the dealer down over the hood of the Bronco. "Shut up," he said. "You have the right to remain silent. Use it."

"I know," Rahner said. "I have the right to an attorney. I know, I know."

"All right," Chitwood said, pulling Rahner's arm off the hood and cuffing the wrist behind his back. "How many more times we gonna do this, Rahner?" He grabbed the man's other arm and cuffed the wrists together.

Rahner said nothing, and Chitwood guided him into the back seat of the Bronco.

He closed the door, then got into the driver's seat, grabbing the mic off the under-dash radio and thumbing it on. "Walsh. Walsh. You out there? I got a ten-sixteen at the Kwik-E Mart. It's Rahner."

From the backseat, Rahner spoke up. "Oh man, not Walsh," he said. "That guy's a fucking weirdo."

# 4

The sky looked bruised and swollen by late afternoon, and it started snowing again. Daniel sat in the chair next to Nancy's bed, watching her sleep, her facial tics betraying a dream that caused her features to twist into a cruel and angry crone that Daniel had never encountered, before relaxing back into the face of the woman he had fallen desperately in love with so many years earlier.

He glanced at the window and the snow falling hypnotically beyond it, and his thoughts drifted once again to the idea of shuffling off this mortal coil, on his own terms.

He thought maybe he'd take that old red K-Car down to the edge of Tillman's Depths and run a hose from the tailpipe to the window. This time of year, there'd be little chance of a good Samaritan happening upon him there. If indeed this town had any good Samaritans left. And if so, they most likely weren't the residents that could still afford to live on lakefront property in Kobbe's End.

"Penny for your thoughts, babydoll?"

He turned to find Nancy smiling wanly at him. "Oh, you know. 'Do fish get thirsty?' 'Did Adam and Eve have belly buttons?' 'Should I bother getting new tires for a car we don't even drive?' That kind of stuff."

"You're a terrible liar."

He shrugged. "Michael stopped by earlier," he said, changing the subject.

"Oh, yeah? How's Michael?"

"Fancy cars and swimming pools," Daniel replied. "He really just came by to let me know I was fired."

Nancy winced, sitting up a little straighter in the bed. "You're kidding me."

"I am not."

"Oh, Danny," she said, reaching for his hand. "I'm so sorry."

He smiled and squeezed her hand gently, afraid of hurting her with even the mildest touch. Her skin was dry, hot, and he wondered if she'd been burning up like this all day. "I'm not. The church has been nothing but an inconvenience these last few months."

"I don't like hearing you say things like that, and I'm sad you feel that way."

The old wireless phone on the nightstand suddenly trilled, and although most likely a telemarketer, Daniel took the opportunity to pick it up gleefully, smiling and dramatically holding up a finger for silence.

Nancy scowled and rolled her eyes.

"Hello," he said into the receiver, and was surprised to hear the panicked voice of Jenny Thomas on the other end.

"Daniel, thank goodness! I need your help!"

"Jenny," he said, and Nancy looked up, also surprised. "What can I do for you?"

"It's Charlotte," the old woman replied. "She's gotten into the yeast rolls!"

Daniel stared blankly at Nancy, who cocked her head at him. "I'm sorry... Charlotte?"

"My dog!"

*Ah, yes. The Pom.*

He sighed, smiling to reassure Nancy. "That actually sounds like more of a veterinary emergency than a religious one."

Nancy made a sour face and smacked him softly on the knee. "Hey," she whispered, so as not to be heard on the other end. "You be nice to your parishioners. Especially the only one who's been a genuine friend to us for the last year."

Daniel gave his wife a pained look, knowing she was right. *I guess there's at least one good Samaritan in this town. And she just volunteered me.*

"Okay, okay," he said into the receiver. "I'll be over in just a bit. No, it's absolutely fine."

He hung up the phone and glared at Nancy. "It is most definitely not absolutely fine."

"But, but, *Chaaarlotte*," Nancy said, pushing out her lower lip for dramatic effect.

"Charlotte," he said, nodding, then turned serious. "I don't like how warm you feel. You sure you're going to be okay tonight?"

"Go," she assured him. "I'm fine."
Daniel did not believe her.

The snow had stopped falling by the time he'd wrestled his boots on and shrugged into his jacket, but the sky was still black and threatening when Daniel finally got on his way.

He trudged through the new snow, appreciating how it had freshened the look of the black slush on the roads and sidewalks he had made his way through this morning.

Jenny Thomas's house was only a mile or so from the church, but the most direct route took him past the homeless encampment next to the hardware store.

He marveled at the sheer number of tents and lean-tos that crowded the lot, all of them covered in a fine dusting of snow. Lights illuminated several of the thin, plastic walls, and he saw what he feared might even be an open flame in one tent.

There was pity at the quality of life on display, but it was tempered with sadness and not a little fear. Crime in the neighborhood had skyrocketed, and the tiny town's law enforcement couldn't hope to keep up with it. Most of these souls weren't even town natives. It was a rough life of poor decisions that saw your journey climax at Kobbe's End.

In contrast, Jenny's house was warm, adorable and inviting, a small rambler with a postage stamp-sized lawn surrounded by a well-kept picket fence.

She fussed about as he removed his puffy winter jacket and boots, impatient with his efforts to keep the slush off her hardwood floors.

When he was ready, she led him to her tidy kitchen, filled with modern appliances that made Daniel wonder (not for the first time) where her money came from. "She's in here," she said.

For a moment, his brain refused to categorize the furry footstool he was looking at as a dog. But that was Charlotte, all right, the tiny Pomeranian that would furiously launch itself at the picket fence if anyone dared walk past her yard.

Only now Charlotte looked like a fur-wrapped balloon, bloated and wobbling on legs that looked too small to support her.

"Ah…" Daniel said, gathering his thoughts. "How did this happen again?"

The woman wrung her hands together. "I started making yeast rolls for Nancy. And I left them in the kitchen to rise before baking. I settled in to watch *December* on Netflix. Have you seen that? The writer that killed his wife and his agent? My goodness, it's terrifying. But when I went to check in on the rolls, the pan was empty! There were twelve!"

Daniel stared at the chubby culprit. "Charlotte ate twelve unbaked yeast rolls?"

"I know!"

The round dog barked at the mention of her name, wondering when she could expect her typical head and chin scratches. She then let a loud fart rip, wobbling a bit with the effort.

A moment later, the smell hit Daniel and he physically recoiled. *Dear God, it smells like rolls.*

Jenny waved a hand in front of her nose. "The burps are even worse," she said. "They smell like Old Charter!"

"What?" Daniel said, and then realized, "Ohhhh. The yeast must be fermenting. Have you called the vet?"

"No answer," she replied. "Heather has the nearest vet, over an hour away on a summer day! With the snow? Who knows?"

Daniel nodded. "They're probably snowed in, too." He pulled his cellphone from within the voluminous pockets of the sweater he had worn underneath his winter jacket. He was pretty oblivious to all the tricks that could be done with it - apps, and all that - but he knew how to Google a problem, and in short order, he was calming his flustered friend down.

"She's probably going to be fine," he told her, reading from the tiny screen in his hand. "Maybe a little drunk. We should probably get some Pepto in her, if you have any."

"I'm guessing she won't like that nearly as much as she enjoyed the rolls."

Daniel chuckled as he bent over and picked up the dog, who groaned loudly. "Charlotte, I know exactly how you feel."


They sat together for a while, keeping an eye on Charlotte as she tried to go about her regular dog routine, burping and farting merrily away - *she does smell like bourbon*, Daniel thought, and *I probably do now, as well* - and they chit-chatted for a bit about true crime books, podcasts and television shows, (Jenny's real passion) over hot cocoa and a delicious tiramisu of her own making. Jenny spoke briefly of the bad dreams and headaches she had been having lately, but poo-pooed Daniel's suggestion to have Matt Carpenter down at the clinic take a look at her; and finally, nearly an hour after he had arrived, Daniel convinced her that Charlotte was going to be fine, and that he had his own loved one at home that also required his care.

He turned down her offer to drive him home, convinced she would insist on visiting with Nancy. He just wasn't willing to tire his wife any more than necessary. Instead, he put on his boots and puffy winter jacket and started his journey home, and if his faith in humanity was not completely restored, then at least it had certainly been nudged in a positive direction.

Nikos DaBronzo poked his head out of the one-person tent he'd set up in between two much bigger tents in the canvas city that had sprung up next to the hardware store.

The sun had gone down an hour ago, and the temperature had plummeted with it. The sky threatened snow again, and he cursed the winter that had just begun, knowing they'd get snow off and on until April.

He stretched, zipped his fuzzy jacket up to his chin, and glanced around the tent city. It was flanked by Morgret & Son's Hardware on one side, a two-story brick building with no windows. On the other side was Carlos', a high-end Mexican steakhouse that had boarded up their dining windows that faced the lot. Whether that was to keep the diners from seeing out or the residents of the tent city from seeing in, Nikos couldn't say. A little of column A, a little of column B, he'd guess.

There were at least thirty tents of various shapes and sizes squeezed into the lot, and many of them were already lit from within, indistinct silhouettes moving in front of halogen light sources as their owners settled in for another frosty night.

He stepped gingerly through the makeshift walking path, over empty cans and disintegrating cardboard boxes crushed by the snowfall, around bicycle parts and engine parts and even clothes dryer parts, winding his way through the maze of canvas homes and avoiding eye contact with any of the other tent city residents that hadn't yet settled in for the night, until he reached the sidewalk.

Most of the homeless residents knew and respected each other. Some of them were out of luck, out of work, and had no family to take them in. Some of them were just nutjobs, legit insane weirdos who simply could not, now or ever, function in society.

But *all* of them seemed to hate Nikos.

It wasn't because of the drugs. Just about everyone here was as guilty as he of waking up, heading out to obtain drugs - whether private or state-funded - and coming back to the lot to sleep the day away.

It wasn't because they thought he was a thief. He *was* a thief, willing to steal just about anything that wasn't nailed down. But again, that description fit most of the residents of the 'End's tent city.

No, they didn't like Nikos because they knew he could just go back home anytime he wished. His mom had come by regularly in the last few months, begging him to come back, no strings attached, just to get out of the cold, get away from the violence and have a hot meal, get his life back together.

But Nikos didn't want to get his life back together. He enjoyed wandering the neighborhoods when everyone was asleep. He liked taking what he wanted, when he wanted.

Strolling the mostly empty streets, trying car door handles, taking anything valuable from anyone stupid enough to leave their vehicles unlocked… this was Nikos's idea of a good time.

Sometimes, if there was nothing of value in an unlocked car, he'd trash the interior as retribution for wasting his time.

That seemed like a likely forecast for tonight. Nikos was sour and on edge. That asshole Chitwood had busted his score earlier today, and Nikos had ditched the smack as soon as he'd seen the red and blues, hightailing it back to the vacant lot and lying low until now.

He was out twenty bucks, no smack, getting a headache, and in the mood to break something.

The sky felt close enough to touch as Daniel shuffled down the slushy roads that led home, and he imagined he could reach right up and get a handful of the thick, black clouds that roiled above him.

His thoughts were on Nancy as he passed the homeless camp. He imagined she would get a chuckle out of *The Tale of Charlotte and the Twelve Yeast Rolls*.

His mood spoiled as he remembered how hot and dry her hand had felt earlier, and the immeasurable pain she had been in for the last week or so, and he picked up his pace, suddenly fearful that perhaps her time on this mortal plane was finally nearing its end.

Daniel had reluctantly come to grips with the idea of Nancy dying, had hated that he sometimes hoped it would come soon and spare her the physical agony she'd suffered lately. Hated even more his own need for her to hang on as long as possible and not abandon him in this bleak and barren existence.

Lost in thought, he didn't notice Nikos until the young man spoke.

"Whoa, whoa, whoa," Nikos said, nearly startling Daniel into a scream.

He choked it down, but his face betrayed his surprise, and Nikos smiled cruelly at it.

"Where you going so fast, old man?"

Daniel put his head down and attempted to hurry past, but the man put a hand on his chest, stopping him.

He looked up at Nikos. *Man? This is just a kid! Maybe not even eighteen!* He dropped his gaze, hating himself, but aware that this burly eighteen-year-old could likely do a fair amount of damage to a slight fifty-five-year-old.

"You got a couple bucks?" Nikos asked.

"Sorry," Daniel said. "I'm not carrying any cash."

Nikos narrowed his eyes. "Bullshit. Just a couple bucks." He leaned towards Daniel and sniffed. "And your booze, too."

Daniel couldn't help but raise his eyes, confused. "Booze? I don't have any booze, either. No cash, and definitely no booze."

"Now I know you're fucking with me," Nikos said. "I can smell the whiskey all over you."

Daniel risked a smile. Maybe he could talk his way out of this. Maybe he could regale the boy with *The Tale of Charlotte and the Twelve Yeast Rolls*. "Look," he began, then got a closer look at the face of the boy that was harassing him. "Nikos? Is that Nikos DaBronzo?"

Nikos squinted back at Daniel, recognition and embarrassment flooding over his face. "Oh hey, Mister Cook," he said with a lopsided grin. "How's it going?"

"Nikos, what are you doing?" Daniel glanced back at the tent city behind them. "Are you living out here? Does your mother know you're out here?"

Nikos's face was burning, the color rising up his cheeks, and Daniel felt a minor victory at that.

"Sorry, Mister Cook. I didn't realize it was you."

The last time Daniel had seen Nikos had to have been a decade ago, when the Sunday School services had finally been canceled. That young boy was virtually unrecognizable in the sharp and cruel features of the man he was becoming, and Daniel felt a stab of guilt at being part of the system that had failed the boy.

But Nikos was backing away now, clearly mortified. "Hey, don't mention this to my mom, okay?"

Daniel nodded, as if doing the boy a favor, feeling it prudent not to mention that the boy's mother, a notorious battle-axe, hadn't seen the inside of the church in many years, either.

Nikos finally turned and sheepishly jogged back toward the tent-covered lot.

Daniel felt his knees go a little weak as the rush of adrenaline abated. This was the closest in his adult life that he'd come to a physical fight, and he wasn't prepared for the nausea that was coming on. His hands trembled as his shoulders loosened, and he stood there a moment longer, gathering his wits, and shaking his head at his luck, wiping away the flop-sweat that was slowly freezing against his forehead.

*Too much excitement for one day,* he thought. *Please, no more.*

# 5

As he approached the church, dark and muted as the gloom of evening neared actual night, his profound lack of interest in the building saddened Daniel. Only a few years earlier, he had still felt eager about serving the community and had loved the sight of the tiny church with its cross on the peak against the sky.

Now, nothing. His faith, already tested by their miscarriages years earlier, had slowly dwindled during the course of Nancy's illness, which had coincided with the town's woes, and then that of the entire world's as it shut down, and now he just felt a mild disdain for the trappings and the Christian imagery. He knew he wouldn't be able to continue his charade much longer.

He circled behind the church and let himself in through the kitchen door, as usual, taking off his hat before realizing that the dark room was illuminated by the open door of the refrigerator.

A dozen thoughts raced and fought for attention and action. His senses, so raw from the earlier encounter with Nikos, started screaming at him:

*Nancy was bedridden.*

*Someone was rifling through his refrigerator in the dark.*

*Crime was up in the neighborhoods surrounding the homeless camp.*

The dots connected themselves, and the only real question he had was how many intruders he was dealing with, and whether Nancy was in any immediate danger. He had an instant to marvel at the difference in his mindset at being assaulted on the street versus his home being invaded, and then, steeling himself, he moved.

He reached blindly on the nearest countertop for the first weapon he could find - a dirty coffee mug that he felt a small satisfaction at not cleaning this morning - while simultaneously flailing at the light switch next to the door and screaming, "What do you want?!?" His voice cracked embarrassingly on the word *you*, but he cocked his arm, ready to release the coffee mug at the assailant with maximum force.

Nancy popped her head over the open refrigerator door, hair a fright, eyes lighting up at the sight of her husband. The delight on her face made her look ten years younger. "I don't know," she said, "But I'm starving!"

Daniel's jaw nearly hit the floor, and he stumbled in his dripping snow boots across the scarred kitchen floor to his wife. "What are you thinking? You shouldn't be out of bed!" He reached out a hand to steady her.

"No," she said, keeping him at bay with one outstretched arm. "No. I'm fine. Really. I'm just..." and then she stumbled a bit. "... really hungry."

Daniel moved in to support her, amazed that she'd had the strength to hold him back at all. She'd been weak as a kitten for the last month.

He helped her to the kitchen table, and she leaned woodenly against him as she sat.

"What's gotten into you?" he asked. "You haven't been out of bed in a month. I can't even remember when you were last downstairs!"

"I know," she said, angry. "And I'm sick of it! Besides, I feel better tonight!" Her eyes were full of fire, and she clutched his forearm. "It feels like, I don't know... like a fever has broken."

Daniel examined her as she spoke, noting the vice grip she had on his arm. She looked healthier, although the mottling that had developed at her temples was still evident.

He held the back of his hand against her forehead for a moment.

*Still warm, but not like earlier...*

She pulled his hand away and smiled at him, but her eyes were desperate, almost pleading.

"Okay," he said, nodding slowly. "Okay. Maybe..." he lost his train of thought. Instead, he said the only thing that made sense to him, "Would you like me to make something for you?"

Her shoulders drooped with relief. "Oh, yes. Please. I really want a steak. Or maybe a burger. I don't care. Something solid."

*the secret language of spiders*

"You got it." He smiled at her as he stood. "One burger coming up."

As he opened the freezer, eyeing the burger patties he had brought home just this morning, she spoke to him:

"It's a miracle, isn't it." It wasn't a question.

He turned back to her, thoughtful. "Maybe it is."

Later, Daniel recounted *The Tale of Charlotte and the Twelve Yeast Rolls* ("Horrible, horrible," Nancy commented as he spoke of Charlotte's gas, all between bites of burger #2), and then *The Ballad of Nikos DaBronzo* ("That DaBronzo kid was a bad seed from day one," she said between mouthfuls of burger #4), and when she finally stood to clear the various dirty dishes from the table, Daniel stood with her, trying to take the plates from her hands. "Let me," he said.

"Daniel Cook," she said, refusing to relinquish her grip. "I can clean up my own mess. Especially after months of you cleaning it up for me."

He released the plates, marveling again at the change in her, at the strength in her hands, and followed her to the sink with the rest of the dishes from the table.

She dropped her plates in the stainless-steel sink, and took Daniel's, clattering them on top, then turned and embraced him so tightly that he found it difficult to breathe. "I can't even explain how amazing it feels to be out of that damned bed," she whispered into the crook of his neck.

He pulled back and smiled at her, leaned in to kiss her softly. She turned the kiss into something deeper, a kiss for a long-lost lover, and he felt himself responding. When they broke, she was grinning up at him…

"Although," she said playfully, "I wouldn't mind getting back to it for a little while…"

Daniel chuckled softly. "I would very much enjoy that. But I think you might be pushing yourself just a bit." He took her hand and led her out of the kitchen. "I think maybe you should rest a little before we decide you've suddenly made a full recovery."

Nancy planted herself in the hall, refusing to be budged. "Danny," she said, making him meet her eyes. "I have been sick - literally bedridden - for months. I feel good tonight, for the first time in a very long time. And I don't know if it means I'm better, or maybe I'm just better for one night… but I want to make love to my husband, and I'm not going to risk losing this chance."

She slid past him in the hallway, still gripping his hand tightly, and then it was her leading him up the stairs to the bedroom, and he could not have stopped her if he had wanted.

They made love slowly, both of them holding the other tightly, almost desperately, and even when they had finished they refused to let go.

# 6

The ruins of Tillman House dominated the shore of the lake that shared its name, a great, black, skeletal stain upon the snowy landscape.

The mansion had mysteriously and legendarily caught fire in 1885, amidst a summer of mayhem and missing persons.

Several town residents disappeared that night, including both Decraine Kobbe and Richard Tillman, and only the body of the town's constable was found, his skull bashed in with a large stone near the edge of the lake.

In 1979, the town decided that the abandoned property would become the Kobbe County Museum and Visitors Center. Fences were erected, thousands of dollars of plans were drawn up, and then movement came to an abrupt halt as money and interest dried up.

Since then, the ruins had become a popular destination for adventure seekers and ne'er do wells, and more than one high-schooler over the years had claimed to have seen the ghosts of Richard Tillman and his beautiful wife, Eva, watching the lake from the third story windows of the gutted house.

Deputy Jeffrey Walsh wasn't concerned with ghosts. He leaned against one of the mansion's charred and mossy timbers and took a long drag off his Marlboro, studying the moonlit surface of the lake in front of him.

He came out here often, parking outside the rusting construction fencing that still surrounded the Tillman property, shimmying through the same gap in the fence that the high school kids had been using to snoop around the ruins of Tillman House since the 70's.

Walsh had joined the Kobbe County Sheriff's when Washington State was throwing out giant signing bonuses in an effort to interest people in joining law enforcement after Defund the Police campaigns had decimated police forces.

An easily passed psych-eval later (he'd been faking personality tests since his teens) and two months in Academy boot camp, and here he was, Deputy Jeffrey Walsh.

He'd originally wanted Seattle or Tacoma, but there was a considerable amount of friction between the police and the public still, and as much as he'd craved immediate action, he didn't relish his activities being put under a microscope right out of the Academy. Instead, he'd responded to the single opening Kobbe County had posted. Secluded. Low cost of living. Good benefits. The only downside had been no real action, mostly desk work.

Anyone could see Kobbe's End was a lost cause, one of many small towns sputtering out in the wake of the pandemic, and Walsh had thought he'd probably made a horrible mistake in relocating here. But shortly after securing his new apartment, he'd experienced his first dream of Tillman's Depths, a real corker that left him cold and sweaty, his cock stiff as marble.

The next night, after finishing his shift, he'd come out to the ruins of Tillman House, surprising a group of teens that had shown up to party. They'd scattered, abandoning their beer, their folding chairs, their Bluetooth speaker, and, he soon discovered, their dog.

After he'd chased the kids off, Walsh had sat on the edge of the shore, much like tonight, studying the lake's glassy surface.

He'd felt a yearning, a longing to cleanse himself in those waters, a familiarity that he couldn't comprehend, a… *a calling*, if you will.

He'd imagined he could hear the heartbeat of the lake that night, felt his own heart skip and try to match it, an odd tempo in three/four time, tribal, almost. Primal. The water seemed to glow with a bioluminescence in the black, starless night.

Walsh remembered vividly how startled he'd been by the sudden cold and wet pressure against his hand, and he let out a shocked yelp that had scared the mutt next to him nearly as bad as the poor pooch had scared him.

He'd stretched his hand back out, letting the spooked dog sniff him, and he noted the collar around the dog's neck.

*Oakley*, read the dog's tags, once it had gotten close enough again to let him scratch its head.

The Deputy scanned the houses around the lake that he could see. He supposed Oakley could have wandered over from any of them, but Walsh had a hunch that the dog belonged to the high-schoolers he'd scared off earlier.

The pull of the lake had snagged the Deputy's attention again as he absentmindedly stroked the dog's fur, and he tried desperately to recall the previous night's dream of the lake's dark waters.

It had been shockingly violent, he knew that, but also maddeningly sexy, and he'd jerked off immediately upon waking.

And as he had gripped the dog's collar firmly and dragged it, wading into the lake with him and holding the struggling mutt under the surface for several minutes, hearing Tillman's Depths' furiously pounding rhythm in his head, Walsh thought that this was very close to what his dream had been about.

That night he'd gone home and masturbated furiously to the memory of the event. He felt re-energized. He had a purpose. He served the lake now, he knew that. Tillman's Depths... or whatever force inhabited it.

And since then, he'd returned to the lake several times, twice bearing gifts.

The first was an orange tabby that had fought him with unbelievable fury, tearing long, deep furrows in his arms before finally flopping still. A month later, he'd brought a stray dog for the lake, thinking perhaps its depths required a larger gift this time, more mass to please his master, and indeed, after that the heartbeat of the lake had become a constant soundtrack to his life, a steady *boom buh-boom* that accompanied him throughout the day, no matter where he was or what he was doing.

He'd been distracted for days afterwards, short with coworkers, leaving work early or missing it completely, and Sheriff Chitwood had finally pulled Walsh into his office one afternoon after an explosive argument.

"Do you like your job, Deputy?" Chitwood had asked him.

Walsh had nodded his head sullenly, knowing where the conversation was heading.

"I don't know what's going on in your personal life," the Sheriff had said, "And I honestly don't care. But you better get it handled, and damn quick. I've got no time for your bullshit. I'll bounce you out of here so fast it'll make your head swim, understand?"

Walsh understood, and he told the Sheriff so, and he'd made sure that Chitwood had nothing to complain about since then as far as his deputy was concerned.

When he'd received his first assignment today – a quick suspect pickup and delivery from the Kwik-E-Mart – Walsh had responded immediately.

He'd transported the suspect – that weirdo Rahner - to the County Jail in the Sheriff's Office, booked him, and then spent the last agonizing hours of his shift on receptionist duty, counting down the minutes until he could escape back to the lake again.

Now, he gazed out past one of the numerous, rusted "Swimming Prohibited" signs and over the dark water. He took another deep drag, watching the smoke and exhalation of his breath in the icy air.

Last night, The Depths had reached out to him via his dreams again, pummeling him with images of needle-sharp teeth, bristly joints and dull, red eyes, and the throbbing triplet beat that was almost a language…

Walsh had awakened this morning knowing he'd end the day at Tillman's Depths, even though was still unsure what the lake demanded of him.

Regardless, he'd come prepared.

Stubbing his cigarette out in the rocky shore and standing, he stretched his back first one way and then the other, then turned and headed towards the plastic pet crate he'd dragged down to the shore from his car, cracking his knuckles in anticipation.

# 7

The next morning, Daniel was surprised to find Nancy in even better spirits, if that were possible. She made him put on his boots and jacket, dragging him out of the house and down to the neighborhood park, which was as deserted and depressing as the rest of the town these days.

The playground toys, which were ancient and in disrepair, made for shapes that were even creepier, Daniel thought, now that they were hidden, covered with snow.

*That's the merry-go-round, and those weird lumps must be the spring-riders. These are the old picnic tables.*

And the statue of the town's founders, Kobbe and Tillman, clad in Union Army garb, was immediately identifiable.

But the playground climber - a six-foot high dome made of crisscrossed iron bars - had transformed into something ethereal and frightening with the snow and icicles that hung from it. There was a nightmarish quality about the déjà vu it invoked in him.

"Isn't it beautiful?"

He turned away and raised his eyebrows at Nancy, who was bundled up against the weather as he was, and beaming so widely that he felt an actual pain in his heart. "You're beautiful," he responded. "I can't believe how quickly you've bounced back."

"Right? It's wonderful. You have no idea how trapped I've felt, stuck in bed all this time." She glanced sideways at him. "I was afraid you'd start bringing more doctors in to look at me."

Daniel sighed, but she had opened the door. "Nancy," he said, keeping his voice light. "I do think we should have you checked out. This is all so sudden, so… bizarre."

Nancy's lips tightened. She was shaking her head before he could even finish. "No. Absolutely not. I won't go back to the hospital again. I won't. Ever."

Daniel said, "We can bring someone to the house…"

"No, Daniel. I mean it."

Frustrated, he appealed one last time. "What if you get sick again? What if this is just temporary?"

*What if I get my hopes up and you go and die on me?*

Nancy's face softened. She leaned into him, wrapping an arm around his waist, squeezing him through both of their jackets. "What if it is?" She looked up at him, her breath visible in the cold. "Danny, two days ago I was praying to God that he would just let me die. I've suffered enough."

Daniel felt a wave of guilt wash over him for his own wishes, his thoughts about Nancy passing quickly so that he could end his own pain.

"What if this is just some final gift we've been given, and I die tomorrow?" she said. "Is that how we should spend my last hours together? With you sitting next to my bed while I get more tests done?"

Daniel felt his eyes filling with tears at the thought, and he blinked them away. "No. That's not how we should spend any more of our time."

She pulled away from him, smiling. "That is the correct answer." And then she ran a gloved hand across the top of a picnic table, gathering up a wad of snow and flinging it at Daniel with a giggle.

The snowball hit him directly in the chest and Nancy laughed as he bent to make his own snowball in retaliation. "Oh, yeah?" he asked, joining in on her laughter. "You sure you want to go down this road?" And he flung his snowball, which Nancy ducked with ease.

She scored another direct hit and laughed wildly. "God," she said, already packing another snowball, "I feel so STRONG!"

The snowball hit Daniel in the shoulder, and he winced from the force of it. But before he could say anything, Nancy was nearly on top of him, eyes sparkling with joy, cheeks ruddy with life. He fell in love all over again. How could he not?

"Let's walk," she said. "I want to see the town."

Daniel groaned. "Okay. But I think you're going to be very disappointed."

They left the park arm in arm, and neither of them noticed the black Tesla sedan that was parked across the street, nor the man within, who was watching them both very closely.

Their walk took them past Morgret & Sons and the lot full of tents, and Daniel watched Nancy's face fall. He decided not to share the fact that the homeless had somehow designated the gutter one block away the public bathroom for the lot's residents.

"Where are they all coming from?" she said, realizing these could not all be displaced residents of Kobbe's End. "And why here? Seattle or Spokane seems a smarter destination. At least there are agencies set up to provide aid. Daniel, we have to do something."

Daniel said nothing, on the lookout for Nikos or any of his associates. Looking out over the tents and trash, he mourned the regular walks and hikes he and Nancy used to take before she'd fallen ill, before Kobbe's End and all the societies of the world had fallen ill.

They continued past Jenny Thomas's house, her empty driveway and the lack of Charlotte charging at them from her side of the fence signaling there was no one home.

Daniel was disappointed, secretly hoping he could convince Nancy to end her exploration here with a friend rather than see what had happened to her town.

His fears were confirmed as they entered the three blocks of Main Street that made up the downtown of Kobbe's End.

The plywood in the window of Migliore's Pizza was warped and split from the last two years' worth of brutal summers and winters. The Migliore's had always threatened to head back to Italy, and had finally made good on the promise when it became apparent that the two-week shutdown they had been forced into would last much, much longer.

Serfling's Floral was dark and empty, and Vanessa's Furniture had burned down last year, the ruins left like a blackened skeleton covered in broken, frozen safety tape. Kobbe's End was unincorporated, and there were simply no volunteers left - or willing - to take care of the mess.

Nancy's spirits had dropped considerably by the time they'd reached Williford's, and Daniel grieved for the town with her, seeing its decay again through fresh eyes.

She surprised him when she spoke. "Let's go to the lake."

"It's a couple miles further," he said. "And you know those roads haven't been plowed."

"Please," she said. "I'd like to see something nice today."

"Of course," he acquiesced immediately, wondering again at her newfound stamina.

Tillman's Depths had a reputation for being haunted, a trait it shared with several deep lakes across the continental United States, but it also had a history to back it up.

The original spider migration the town celebrated every year had ended at the lake, according to legend, and both Decraine Kobbe and Richard Tillman were feared to have disappeared in its dark waters a few years later, their bodies never recovered. The two men were often discussed in hushed tones and wild speculations of the murder and madness that led to the burning of Tillman House on the Depths' shore.

In the years since the town's founders' disappearance, several gigantic houses had appeared on the far shore of the lake, but most sat empty today, abandoned after the mines had run dry.

The gravel path that wound through the woods surrounding the lake had nearly eight inches of frozen, untouched snow upon it; less than the rest of the town because of the tall, dark forest that flanked both sides of the trail. Even in the town's glory days, there would have been little reason for anyone to come to the lake in this weather. As they chugged through the snow, Daniel half-joked that it might have been easier to take the abandoned logging road that led directly to the old make-out spot near Tillman House.

Daniel walked to the edge of the shore, his breath coming cold and heavy from the effort of dragging his feet through nearly two miles of snow, his thoughts of the last time he and Nancy had been at the lake, early in the year. They'd packed a picnic lunch and had driven up on a surprisingly warm spring day, talking and laughing and eating the rosemary bread from Handelman's Bakery, and since the lake was deserted, Nancy had stripped to her underwear and bra, laughing at Daniel's surprised look and slipping into the frigid water after hanging her clothes on one of the many "Swimming Prohibited" signs that were posted around the lake.

She'd laughed and squealed loudly at the temperature of the water, enduring it only long enough to get a few strokes in before giving up and using their picnic blanket to dry herself off, while Daniel kept watch to make sure they weren't found out.

It was perhaps their last good memory of the year. Nancy fell ill a few days later, and their lives changed drastically.

She'd grown quiet as they'd approached the lake today, and Daniel wondered if she was recalling that same spring memory. He'd struggled to keep up with her as she moved faster, almost urgently, through the snow.

*With purpose*, he thought.

He'd called out to her to wait for him, but she continued on. Perhaps the crunching snow under her feet had drowned out his voice.

Now, she stood at the very edge of the lake, the soles of her thick winter boots cracking through the thin crust of ice that had formed where the water met the rocky shore.

He noted that her breath came sure and easy, the trek through the snow having had little effect on her.

Nancy's eyes were focused on the center of the dark lake, but she finally turned towards Daniel, a mix of frustration and concentration clouding her features, as if she were trying to identify a fragment of a tune that danced just out of reach.

"Can you hear that?"

Daniel tried to calm his breathing, straining to catch what she was hearing. "No," he said. "What is it?"

"I don't know," she said, turning her ear towards the lake. "It sounds like… a hum, I guess? But with a beat. Singing, maybe? Haunting… like a smile at midnight."

"Maybe music from across the lake," Daniel offered, but the houses they could see on the far shore looked dark, maybe vacant.

He studied the buildings a quarter mile across the lake's still, black surface. He could see the charred ruin of Richard Tillman's mansion, untouched since its destruction more than a hundred years earlier. But then something that Nancy had just said started to bother him. He turned towards her. "Like a smile at-" he began, then stopped short.

Nancy had waded nearly knee-deep into the icy water and looked like she had no intention of stopping.

"Hey!" Daniel shouted, rushing towards her. "What are you doing?"

The splashing of his boots startled her out of her daze, and her eyes widened, confused as he took hold of her elbow and steered her back to the snowy shore.

"What's going on?" he asked her, his voice low and cautious.

"I'm… I'm not sure."

He searched her eyes, but she turned away, embarrassed. "Nance?"

She met his eyes then, afraid.

*That makes two of us.*

"Let's get home," he said, feeling his legs and feet aching already from the icy water that had soaked through his boots and pants. "We'll catch frostbite if we wait here."

They came home and stripped out of their wet and freezing clothing, and Daniel rubbed their legs dry after a painfully hot shower, relieved to see no signs of frostbite. They both avoided discussing her spell, tumbling into bed and wrapping themselves around each other until they fell asleep.

That night, Daniel dreamed that he and Nancy were wading into the dark water of Tillman's Depths. They seemed much older than their current ages, perhaps in their seventies, and they were both naked, skinny dipping under a full moon that reflected off the lake's glassy surface.

Nancy was gliding effortlessly through the black water, while he felt himself struggling, his limbs getting heavier and heavier with the exertion.

She swam past him with a smile

*at midnight*

then dunked under, and as he trod the water with more and more difficulty, he turned around and around, waiting for her to resurface, waiting, his anxiety growing as the strength faded from his limbs, still waiting…

But she never came back up.

Nancy opened her eyes to a darkness exploding with colors, scents, and sounds.

Next to her, Daniel was fast asleep, breathing deeply, his closed eyelids twitching as his eyes roamed back and forth in dream.

She turned to face him in the bed, fascinated by the movement of his eyes. She could almost hear them flicking from side to side, and she wondered briefly what he was dreaming about.

From outside she heard a soft beat, as if a car radio were playing an old waltz on the next block over.

But that didn't feel quite right to her.

Nancy slipped easily out of the bed without waking Daniel. She felt a breeze against her nude body.

But that wasn't right, either.

*Not a breeze. Not exactly.*

A *wave* of some kind, a wave that brushed against the hair on her arms without quite touching them.

Silently crossing the floor, she stood at the window that looked over the townhouse's backyard and the alley beyond.

The beat was stronger here, a triplet that felt like it might actually knock the window from its frame, the same beat she'd heard earlier at the lake, and Nancy dropped a hand to the sill to see if it was shaking as much as she thought it must be.

*the secret language of spiders*

The world outside, blue and black and gray and white moments earlier, was now a kaleidoscope of colors exploding across her fingertips.

The snow falling outside the window crunched as it landed and Nancy shivered at the vibrations climbing up her arms.

Something was thundering down the alley, coming closer and closer, and Nancy leaned against the window to see what it might be, a herd of elephants or perhaps rhinos, something that might explain what was making such a racket.

She turned back to Daniel in the bed, sure he'd been roused, sure that the small TV on the wall must be ready to topple.

Her husband snored softly, a thunder crack in her head that snapped her out of her own trance, and suddenly the world was dark and muted again.

Nancy turned back to the window in time to catch two raccoons wandering down the alley in search of a garbage can lid that wasn't frozen tight, and then there was nothing again, not even the faint *bum buh-bum* that had woken her up.

# 8

The next morning, Daniel woke to an empty bed, surprised that Nancy had slipped out without waking him. He attributed it to his exhaustion from the trek to and from the lake.

Slipping on his worn blue-and-white pajamas, he headed downstairs, not bothering to address the heroic mop atop his head.

He found Nancy sitting at the kitchen table and felt his body immediately tighten at the sight. She was wrapped in her gray flannel nightgown, sullen, the joy from yesterday nowhere to be seen.

"Good morning," he said cautiously. "How are you feeling today?"

She shrugged, saying nothing.

He paused at the sink, noting her temples, which looked swollen, angry. *Painful.* "Nancy? You okay?"

Her eyes shifted to him, almost annoyed. "Hungry," she said, "but nothing sounds good to me."

"I'd be surprised if we have any food left, anyway," Daniel said, attempting a chuckle, but inside he was screaming, *This is* exactly *what I was worried about!* "We've cleaned out the cupboards over the last couple of days."

Nancy's eyes stayed on him, unreadable, uncomfortable. He forced a smile.

"I could make some pancakes," he offered.

She shook her head. "I don't know what I want." Her hands clenched and unclenched in frustration. "Definitely not pancakes. Something, I don't know… meaty. But…" she gave up, unable to identify the craving.

Daniel said, "We still have a little bacon. Bacon and eggs?"

She propped her elbows on the table, dropped her head into her hands, near tears. "Sure."

He opened the 'fridge and pulled out the last of the brown paper-wrapped bacon, watching her closely.

*She was right. Yesterday we were given a gift.*


Nancy sat listlessly while the bacon sizzled in the frying pan, answering Daniel's attempts at small talk with shrugs and noncommittal grunts.

When he brought two plates of bacon and eggs to the table, she said nothing, and he asked, "Toast?"

"No."

"Juice? Tea? Water?"

She stared at him balefully. "No."

He sat then, his smile beginning to fail, and jammed a forkful of eggs into his mouth to fight the uncomfortable silence.

Nancy took her own fork and stabbed at the eggs with little interest. Finally, she broke a piece of bacon off between her teeth and chewed it joylessly.

Daniel weighed his options, decided there was no good time, and cleared his throat softly. "I think maybe it's time we discussed-"

She spat the bacon out of her mouth and slammed her fist down, her hand accidentally catching the edge of her plate and sending everything flying.

Daniel's eyes went wide as the bacon and eggs flipped through the air, the plate landing hard and shattering on the kitchen floor.

He sat stock-still, stunned at what had just happened, a little afraid of the tiny woman across the table.

She glared with angry, frightening eyes that did not recognize him, looking very little like the woman he had shared a snowball fight with just yesterday. And then her face crumpled and she began to sob. "God, I'm so *HUNGRY!*"

Daniel got up and came around the table, kneeling on the floor next to her so that he could snake his arm around her waist. "Sweetheart. Talk to me. What's going on?"

She swiped at the tears spilling down her face, but the dam had burst. "I don't know," she said between sobs. "I ate so much and I'm still hungry! I'm hearing things. I'm feeling things. Throughout the church. Even outside the church! Danny, *I can feel what's happening outside the church!*"

Daniel didn't know what she meant, but it scared him. This sounded like a mental break of some kind. Nancy sounded confused about her surroundings. He held her tight and let her sob into his shoulder. "Shh. Shh," he said. "It's okay. Everything's going to be okay. We're going to the doctor, right now, and we're going to find out what's going on."

He expected some kind of pushback, was prepared to fight her on it if he had to.

"Okay," she said, nodding, and he knew then it must be very bad.

*She's terrified.*

"Okay," he said, standing. "Let's get dressed and we'll head to the hospital." *The nearest hospital is in Sunset*, he thought. But Kobbe's End had its own GP, Matt Carpenter, who was only a few miles down the road. All things considered, Daniel felt Nancy needed attention as quickly as possible.

He helped her to stand, but then she froze. Her eyes, still full of tears, locked on his left knee like a laser. He followed her line of sight to a bloody stain on the knee of his pajamas. He'd knelt on a sharp shard of the broken plate, oblivious to the pain even now, more concerned with Nancy's well-being.

That entire knee of the pajamas was stained dark red, and he had a moment to think about how Dr. Carpenter might not realize who needed treatment when they pulled up.

As he straightened, he watched Nancy's eyes follow the crimson stain, and he tried to pull her to a full standing position, but she was immoveable. "It's nothing," he said. "It'll be fine. Let's -"

Nancy tackled him with sudden fury, her mouth latching onto his knee, her arms and legs wrapping around his body as they tumbled to the kitchen floor together, another shard of broken plate digging painfully into Daniel's back as they slid across the bits of eggs and bacon.

"Nancy! Stop it! What the hell! Stop!" He put his hand against her forehead, shocked at her strength. He couldn't budge her, and she clutched him tighter, her teeth digging through the fabric of the pajamas and breaking skin. He shrieked in pain as his entire pajama leg suddenly soaked through with blood.

*this is not happening*

He cocked his fist back and then began to beat on the head and face of the woman he loved, the pain and shock driving him to anger and defense over all else.

*i'm going insane*

She took no notice, her mouth loosening from his leg for only a moment to find a bigger, better purchase for her teeth, her limbs tightening around him as they continued to struggle.

Grabbing the side of the oven, he was able to pull himself up for a few seconds, desperate to find some leverage, but his hands were slick with his own blood and could find no purchase. He slipped, knocking against the handle of the frying pan as she pulled him back to the floor, the pan falling down after him and landing painfully on his head.

"Fuck!" He saw stars, but reached his hand around and found the handle of the pan, swinging the flat side of it down directly on Nancy's head with an almost comical "BONG!".

*this CAN NOT be happening*

The blow had loosened her grip, and Daniel got his right leg up near her shoulder and gave a mighty shove, flinging her away from him. He scrambled to his feet, adrenaline pumping through his veins, still gripping the dirty frying pan, the pain in his leg sharp and immediate and the floor slippery with food and grease and blood.

Nancy struggled to stand, dazed, her mouth hanging open, breathing heavily, her chin and her teeth smeared with her husband's blood.

*dear Christ what's happened to her EYES*

They were monstrous, wide and inhuman. The kitchen bulb reflected dully off the red-black spheres that filled her eye sockets. No white, no pupil, just round, alien orbs where his wife's beautiful brown eyes had been only moments ago.

She studied him for a moment, head cocked, shoulder heaving with each labored breath, and for a brief second he could see that she was confused, as bewildered as he was as to what had just happened, and somehow, seeing a glimmer of his wife in the face of this unnatural thing was far more horrific than anything else that had just happened.

Daniel swung the frying pan at her again, a grand-slam kind of swing, connecting with Nancy's face hard enough to send her reeling back against the basement door. It splintered at the lock like the crack of a pistol. The door slammed open, casting her ass-over-teakettle down the rickety wooden steps and into the gigantic basement below the church.

Daniel, bleeding heavily, limped to the broken door at the top of the stairs and stared down at the body of his wife, illuminated by a strip of light from the kitchen, sprawled and immobile on the ancient cement floor below.

# 9

"Looks like you're having yourself a nice dinner tonight."

Daniel blinked, his mind careening back to the present. Blood pooled around the freshly sawed-off steak and then the butcher deftly wrapped brown paper around it, cutting a length of string and tying it neatly.

"That's the plan," Daniel said, faking enthusiasm.

*the secret language of spiders*

"Daniel!"

He stiffened, turning quickly, guilty as a cat on a countertop, his leg throbbing painfully, his mind on the edge of cracking wide open in front of everyone in Williford's supermarket. His smile felt so forced that he feared his face would crack open as well, just crack into a million shards, like the plate that was still shattered all over his kitchen floor.

But there was no "everybody" in Williford's to see it, just Jenny Thomas, who was pushing her cart up next to him, one wheel squeaking rhythmically.

Daniel felt a muscle in his right eyelid start to flutter and twitch, beating faster and faster. "Hello," he said, realizing how robotic and phony he sounded, but unable to remember how he used to sound. *Say something human.* "How is Charlotte today?"

"Oh, much, much better, thank you. Thank you so much for coming over."

He fumed silently, his mind screaming. What if he hadn't been called away to deal with that damn dog and her digestive issues? Would he have seen Nancy suddenly get out of bed for the first time in over a month? Would he have noticed something that might shed a light on what might make her decide that his leg - pajama and all - would be a fantastic meal this morning? For a moment, he hated Jenny Thomas and her dog more than anything in the entire world.

He nodded, his smile incandescent. "Of course."

"How's Nancy feeling? I'd really like to swing by this afternoon, if I may."

Daniel's heart skipped a long beat, and he thought that if he were having a heart attack in the middle of

Williford's, he really hoped it was going to be a catastrophic widow maker, but it appeared he had no such luck. "Oh, no. No. No. Not today. She's taken a turn for the worse, I'm afraid. Not feeling herself at all."

This was almost a lie. In fact, when he had left her, after she had regained consciousness on the basement floor, she had been more or less herself again, not the red-eyed demon he'd sent tumbling down those old stairs.

But she'd started rummaging through all the boxes and furniture in that dark and dank basement, ignoring his pleas for a doctor and sending him out to pick up the freshest, bloodiest meat he could find. When he balked, her eyes flashed angrily and she just said, "*Hurry.*"

Jenny's lips formed a tiny 'o', her eyes widening with genuine concern. "Oh, no. I'm sorry to hear that. I would really love to bring something by, though. For the both of you. Maybe something sweet?"

"No!" He was shocked at the volume of his own voice, quieted himself immediately. "No. She's such a proud woman, you know. She'd be very uncomfortable for anyone to see her in this, ah, weakened condition. Can't keep a thing down, either. Really, anything you made would just be wasted right now."

Jenny was visibly pained at the thought. "That's awful," she said.

The butcher, who had a particularly poor sense of timing, chose this as the moment to slap the giant package of steak on the counter next to Daniel. "Good eatin'," he said with a wink.

Daniel's smile never faltered, and he wondered if perhaps he'd be saddled with this fake grin forever.

*At least my eyelid has stopped twitching.*

He shrugged, holding the gigantic slab of meat out for Jenny to admire. "Whereas I, on the other hand, could eat an entire cow." He pretended to struggle with the weight of the steak for a moment, grinning like a madman. He *felt* like a madman. "Obviously."

And then he nodded awkwardly, pivoting toward the registers, leaving Jenny Thomas very confused and curious about what was going on with her friend and his wife.

# part two:

# the secret language of spiders

# I

*That's going to leave a mark.*

Nancy probed gingerly at the top of her head where Daniel had walloped her with the frying pan.

*I'm probably lucky to be alive.*

Lucky? The blow and the fall had cleared the red fog she'd been under, but the hunger was even worse, a gnawing, living thing in her belly that seemed to be growing exponentially.

She tugged on the length of chain she'd found in an oily box at the corner of the basement, a relic of the time she and Daniel had pulled out the old cedar stump from the backyard with the help of a much larger congregation. The chain was now secured around the basement's single wood support beam with a padlock whose key had been lost to time.

*That's not the important end, anyway.*

The other end of the heavy chain – *the important end* – she'd looped through the old canvas dog collar that had belonged to their border collie Roscoe a decade ago. Roscoe's weathered tags still hung from it, his name and the address of the church mostly rubbed away by the years. The dog had escaped his collar regularly to roam the neighborhood, but she had fastened it around her own neck just loose enough so that she could breathe easily, but still tight enough that it couldn't slip past her chin.

The thick support beam was nearly centered in the huge church basement, which took up the entire footprint of the church and their living space, and the heavy grade chain gave her about twelve feet of roam in any direction, but not enough to reach the bottom of the stairs… which was important to her.

The air was chilly and smelled like dusty mittens - the old cardboard boxes that were filled with ancient magazines, holiday decorations, and business files that probably should have been tossed away during the last seven year cycle.

Her brain was on fire again, thoughts and memories and emotions all crowding over each other in a jagged mosh-pit of *NOW* and *HERE* and she was finding it more and more difficult to concentrate on anything but her growing hunger.

*Hurry up with that food, Danny-boy. I'm begging you.*

She explored some of the more tender areas on her face, grimacing at the thought of what it must look like right now. Daniel had landed a few good licks on her, which was surprising – she didn't know he had it in him.

Nancy knew he'd be pushing to get her into the doctor's as quickly as possible, and she knew she'd have to shut that conversation down immediately. After spending five months in a hospital room in Heather, there was no way she'd willingly go back. No way they could afford it, either.

Besides, she didn't just feel better. She felt great. She felt strong, and she wasn't going to let that strength go. She felt absolutely *amazing*, and *aware*, ready to take on the world.

But God, she was hungry.

For a moment, she was swamped by immeasurable guilt over attacking Daniel in the kitchen, but that was almost immediately swept aside by the memory of how delicious he had tasted and the need to *get that leg back in her mouth again.*

Horrified, she pressed her fist firmly against one of the more prominent bruises that was forming on her face, the pain breaking through that encroaching red fog and bringing tears to her eyes and a measure of clarity.

She wiped the tears away, noting the sandpaper feel of her fingers now. What the hell was happening to her? Everything felt different. Everything was changing.

In the basement corner, something shifted, perhaps as a result of her rooting through all those boxes to find the chain and collar that was now wrapped around her throat.

Her thoughts went sharp again, angular, and she dropped to a crouch, spreading her hands and laying them softly upon the broken concrete floor.

Again the world revealed itself to her through her fingers, a symphony of vibrations that came to her as a combination of sound and color and smell and even emotion. She could feel the fluttering heartbeat of a rat in the corner, hiding in a nest of church brochures it had shredded, itself connected primally enough to its surroundings to know that it was imperative to be silent right now and avoid detection.

*It's not enough, little rat.*

But then another vibration came, an intrusion from something further out as her senses expanded. The rat was close, yes, here in the basement with her, but she could feel the surrounding church, a web of brick and plaster and two-by-fours, insulation and wiring and drywall and carpet, and all of it had its own sound and color; and beyond that, the yard surrounding the church, the trees, the fence, and in the snow-covered lawn out there, a movement, a regular beat that was coming closer, closer…

Upstairs, the kitchen door opened, a small sound, but today it echoed like a shotgun blast through her fingers and she fell backward, snapping out of the trance and the magical world that had enveloped her.

She turned and found Daniel at the top of the old wooden stairs, silhouetted by the daylight of the kitchen above.

"Nancy?"

She dragged the chain with her as she backed towards the basement wall, trying to keep as much distance as possible between her and the man she loved so dearly.

"I'm coming down," Daniel said, his voice catching just a bit. "I've got… food."

He slowly made his way down the staircase, each step a bass drumbeat against her body, and she moved involuntarily forward, clutching with both hands the beam she was chained to.

She could smell the cold package in his hands *smell it through every follicle on her body* and over that, a much warmer, insistent odor, coming from the knee he had rushed to patch up before he left. But more than that, it was just the smell of him... *existing* in front of her.

"Nancy," he said, his voice hopeful as he reached the floor with a thunderous BOOM. "I did what you asked."

"I know," she said, uncomfortable with how guttural and desperate her voice sounded. "I can smell it." She noted the change in his features as his eyes adjusted to the basement gloom, taking in everything – the chain, the support beam, her face, bruised and swelling from his own hand. There was pity. And a deep sadness. And surprise

*relief*

at the chain and padlock.

"I don't think chaining yourself to the basement is the way to deal with this," he said evenly. "Let me take you to the hospital -"

"I'm not going to the hospital, Daniel," she said, knowing how ridiculous that must sound to him. Did she think this would just blow over? That she would suddenly snap out of this after trying to kill

*eat*

her husband in the kitchen?

Of course not. She understood that this was the next step in whatever horrific journey her body had begun almost a year ago. But none of the specialists had shed light on what was going on with her – "cellular degeneration" is all they could fall back on – and she didn't think that this new wrinkle was going to magically help them crack the case.

She had come to terms with the illness early in its course, believing that all things happen for a reason. Now, God willing, perhaps she would find out what that reason was.

Daniel opened his mouth to speak, but Nancy raised her hand, silencing him. Her fingers seemed strange now, longer, as if they had somehow gained another knuckle, and the flesh surrounding them had discolored, mottled like the strange new markings around her temples. "Give me the meat," she said.

He started walking towards her but stopped when she twitched, her eyes frantic.

"Just throw it!" She tried to hide behind the support beam, as if it could protect him from her insatiable hunger. "I don't want to hurt you again."

Pained, he froze where he was. "Nancy, don't. It was an accident-"

"Ha!" she barked. "That wasn't an accident. I wanted to hurt you. I wanted to-"

*eat you*

"-hurt you." She turned away, unable to meet his eyes.

Daniel fought his own tears. "Okay," he said. "Here." He tossed the paper-wrapped package underhand towards her, and Nancy reached out and snagged it effortlessly before it could fall to the floor.

She snapped the twine and tore the paper open, feeling the change in her brain again, less than human but more connected to the world, to the universe, and she reveled in how powerful it made her feel after being bedridden for the last nine months.

Pulling the bloody steak free, she sunk her teeth into it, her hunger stabbing like a white-hot lance through the center of her gut. Even her teeth felt different now, longer, sharper, as if her gums had receded to nothing, and when she chomped on that cold, lifeless meat, her fury was instant and all-consuming.

She spat the offending bite out, throwing the rest of the steak aside. It slapped wetly against one of the numerous cardboard boxes and fell to the concrete floor.

"NO!" she roared, snarling at Daniel, who took a fearful step back. The act infuriated her. "No, no, NO! This isn't right! *THIS ISN'T RIGHT!*"

Daniel flinched at her volume and took another step back. "What's wrong? I did everything you asked!"

The fear in his voice activated that alien thing that was growing within her, and she tried with all her might to push it down, to explain to him *she was starving, couldn't he understand that?* And she didn't know what was happening to her, but she knew the bloody steak tasted awful, and his bloody *knee* tasted absolutely wonderful, and how was she supposed to communicate that without sounding like a complete monster?

As human words failed her and she fell to her knees with a hopeless sob, her senses suddenly sprang to life again.

Every hair on her body fed her an unending stream of information, and what humanity was left inside of her shrank from the onslaught.

The basement's secrets were laid bare to her, the boxes, the knick-knacks, the old propane barbecue in one corner, the nearly unused treadmill in another.

A dozen feet in one direction was Daniel, torn between wanting to comfort his wife, fearful of the new thing she was becoming. A part of her wanted to beg him to stay back, but that bristly new intelligence inside her coiled muscles in anticipation of pouncing as soon as he stepped within range.

In the opposite corner of the room, sudden movement vibrated up through her fingers and she turned, releasing her energy in an explosive leap towards that instead.

From out of the pile of boxes, the basement rat had found the lure of the discarded steak near its nest too much to resist, and as its tiny claws scrabbled on the concrete floor, sending impossibly loud vibrations through Nancy's body, she snatched it up in both hands with a movement almost too fast for the eye to follow.

Clamping her jaws around the rat before it had even registered the danger, she finally found satisfaction as her teeth came together somewhere in the middle of its fat body, its bones cracking, blood raining from the corners of her mouth as she quickly chewed.

She could feel Daniel watching, the horror radiating from him in waves almost as thunderous to her as his quick footsteps backward, and she instinctively froze mid-chew, the rat's tail spasming one last time as all systems failed.

And then he was retching, scrambling up the basement stairs, loudly, clumsily…

*Like a human.*

# 2

A wave of nausea hit Daniel at the top of the stairs and he lurched forward, desperate to pass out amongst the blood, grease, and shattered plate on the kitchen floor rather than risk toppling backwards and down into the basement. He feared he might survive a fall down the stairs… But not whatever came next.

He could still hear Nancy dining on the rat down there, a wet, crunching soundtrack to the darkness creeping in on the edge of his vision.

Stepping gingerly around plate shards, bits of scrambled egg, and tacky, drying blood, he limped to the kitchen sink, turned on the cold tap, and splashed water on his face, fighting the urge to vomit, rinsing the sheen of fear-sweat from his brow and neck.

*This is too much. This is too much for any man, much less me. She needs a professional.*

He turned the faucet off, reaching for a hand towel. He could hear nothing from the basement now.

*And what would a professional do?* he wondered. *Well, sedate her first, I suppose. She's far too dangerous like this.* He turned back to the gaping maw of the basement, with its broken lock and splintered door. *What would that look like? Police in combat armor dragging her body to an ambulance while the neighborhood watched? And then what? A padded room? Tests, certainly. They'd want to know about those crazy fucking eyes, that's for sure. That's going to make the cover of Science Journal, no doubt about it.*

A deep sigh escaped him, and he dried his face and neck, bowing his head sincerely for the first time in months.

*You know, I don't much believe in you anymore.* Probably not the best way to begin a prayer, but he continued on. *If you're real, you're one sadistic son of a bitch. But I could use some guidance right now. I could sure as hell use a sign or-*

"Hello? Daniel?"

His eyes grew wide with panic. Michael's voice had come from the church hall.

Daniel glanced at the bloody mess on the floor and the broken jamb of the basement door, and he quickly dragged a hand through his sweat-damp hair, moving out of the kitchen to head his old friend off.

He rushed into the church hall, faking a smile that faltered when he saw his friend had not come alone.

Standing on the faded runner between the old pews was Michael and a giant of a man in his late 30s, a well-dressed bruiser.

Daniel had a moment to take in the size of the man - he knew several Christian leaders who worked out, even boxed, but this guy looked like a professional wrestler - and then the giant was smiling with too-white teeth and extending a hand towards him.

He accepted the bone-crushing handshake with a bewildered glance at his friend. "Michael," he said. "You should have called. You *really* should have called."

"I did," Michael said. "About an hour ago. There was no answer, so I took a chance."

"Ah," Daniel said, smiling once again. *Nothing wrong here.* "I was out shopping-"

*for raw, bloody steak. you see, my wife is chained in the basement because I think she is turning into a… into a…*

"-for dinner."

Michael nodded, brushing the excuse aside, and introduced the man who was still pumping Daniel's hand. "Daniel, this is Peter Rawlik."

The name rang a bell, but Daniel couldn't quite place it. He smiled and said, "Hello," as he wrestled possession of his hand back.

"I hope we're not intruding," Peter asked.

"Actually," Daniel said, taking advantage of the question, "My wife is quite ill, and-"

Michael held up both hands to stop him mid-sentence. "Daniel, Peter is a doctor with the church in New York, but he's just returned from a long stint in Africa."

*Ah, yes,* Daniel realized. *Peter Rawlik, the specialist I told you I did NOT want here. Thank you so much.*

Daniel fought to keep his face neutral. "Oh. I'm not sure what that has to do with me?"

"Mister Cook," Rawlik said, "Michael told me about your wife's... condition. I know the doctors have been no help, but I've actually come across a case in Africa that is remarkably similar."

"I somehow doubt that."

The doctor blinked and almost smiled. "Still, I wonder if I might visit with her a little, maybe take a blood sample?"

Daniel opened his mouth, then paused.

*This is what you just asked for. Someone to help, someone to shoulder the burden. You trust Michael. Tell them everything. Show them the kitchen and the blood splintered door frame. Bring them down to the basement - just the bottom of the stairs, of course - and watch them... what? Recoil in horror? Call the police, at the very least. They'll lock her away, maybe in a prison, but more likely a facility of some sort, where you'll never be able to see her again. Is that what you want? Are you prepared to never see Nancy again?*

"Absolutely not," he said, so quietly that the men didn't hear him at first. "Absolutely not," he repeated, and this time his voice was strong and sure.

Both Michael and Rawlik stepped back, and Daniel felt a smug sense of satisfaction at their reactions. *I told you no, Michael, and you thought you'd just show up anyway and I'd fold, didn't you?* And he had to admit to himself that he probably would have done exactly that, prior to this morning's events. Just broken down like a cheap shotgun, especially at the size of Rawlik. *But Mikey, things have definitely changed since then.*

Rawlik appealed. "Daniel. I don't think you understand. I'm not just a doctor, I'm an expert on ancient religions. And-"

Daniel made an obvious point of ignoring the big man, turned back to Michael, instead. "How dare you," he said. "How dare you come back here with this man when you know what she's been through, how she feels about doctors and tests and needles and hospitals. When I told you NO."

Michael dropped his eyes, but Rawlik soldiered on. "Really," the doctor tried again. "Just a few -"

"No. She spent five months under constant supervision in the hospital this year." Daniel's fury rose, and he enjoyed being able to finally release all the pain and frustration of the last several months. "You're an 'expert'? You're a 'specialist'? Then you can join the dozen other specialists that visited with her and get the hell out. I won't have her treated like this. Not anymore. I won't."

"Daniel," Michael started, and it sounded like an apology was coming, but Daniel would have none of it. He was on a roll.

"Get out," he hissed.

Michael finally nodded, chagrined, put a hand to Peter's elbow to guide him out.

But the doctor shrugged away from him, and to Daniel, he held out a business card and said, "I'm sorry to have bothered you. Please, Google me. I can help, and I'll be ready for your call."

Michael reached for the doctor's elbow again, this time with a firmer grip. "Come on," he said, meeting Daniel's eyes. "I'm so sorry. I'll call later."

Daniel closed his eyes, pushing the anger down, trying to regain his composure, and when he opened them again, it was just in time to see the church doors closing after his guests. On the floor in front of him was the business card Rawlik had dropped.

In the basement, Nancy, who had heard the entire conversation through every hair on her body, continued to listen as Michael and this new doctor clomped down the outside steps, out of the churchyard, and into Rawlik's black sedan, where she found she could hear them no longer.

# 3

Nancy gripped the basement's wooden center beam, trying to ground herself and pay attention to the sound of Daniel's voice.

In the two days since she'd last eaten that gloriously delicious rat, she and Daniel had started many discussions, him sitting on the basement's bottom step, as he was now, just beyond the reach of the chain she was collared to, and her clinging to the wooden beam like a lifeboat on the black sea of infinity, trying not to think of the blood she could hear coursing noisily through his veins.

Each day, her hunger grew. She could feel her humanity slipping away, replaced by the thing that was taking over her mind, a thing that was made of vibrations and beats; a squirrel on the tree outside, the crunch of tires in the snow at the nearest intersection.

Each time, she begged and cajoled her mind to return and was amazed at how far it had traveled, and the urge to push it further and farther was impossible to resist.

"Maybe we could try something fresher," Daniel said, breaking her trance.

She'd been staring longingly at his leg, and she forced her eyes away, trying not to think about it. "That's not working," she said, pulling at the neck of her gray nightgown, stiff where the rat's gore had dribbled from her chin. "The butcher shop is not working."

She was tired of saying it. They'd tried meat as fresh as it could be delivered, to no avail. The cuts could come straight from the farm, and she knew it still wouldn't be fresh enough.

*Just let me loose on that farm myself,* she thought, and an image sprang into her mind, a fantasy of her at night, climbing the outside of a locked barn and feeling the fearful heartbeats of the cows and pigs and horses inside as they realized there was a predator come for them, and she nearly moaned with desire.

"But what about roadkill?"

Nancy snapped back to reality, narrowing her eyes, hating him for the suggestion.

"Hear me out," Daniel continued, realizing how awful it sounded. "A raccoon is killed at least twice a week on the roads around here. With our weather right now, they'd be frozen solid. I could bring them back here for you-"

"No." She could see the frustration in his heartbeat.

"Or," he said, standing up and sending a wave of air ripples across her follicles and causing her muscles to brace involuntarily. "We could get you to the doctor. Dammit, Nancy, this is ridiculous. Look at you! Look at your skin!"

"I'm not going back to the doctor," she nearly shouted. "How exactly do you think that would go?"

"I don't know," he shouted back. "But at least they'd feed you!"

She didn't quite believe that. She'd gone along with Daniel's experiments because she could see how much he was trying to help her. But she knew what her body was craving... and it required a heartbeat.

"Danny," she hissed. "I'm not going back to the hospital. And if you try to make me... or you get someone else to try to make me... somebody is going to get hurt."

Daniel put his head in his hands, exasperated. "What about Michael's friend?" he asked. He fished Rawlik's crumpled business card out of his back pocket. "He said he'd seen a case like yours before."

She snorted. "Sure he has. Look at me." She held up her long, spidery fingers. "Don't be foolish, Danny."

"Then what?"

She struggled to ignore the colors and vibrations washing over her from the squirrel in the tree outside the church and leveled her eyes at him.

"I have an idea."

# 4

It only took Daniel a couple of days to get the hang of trapping live squirrels from the church's backyard.

The snow and frozen ground were certainly helpful in driving the hungry animals toward the bait in the wire cage trap, but the MVP of the trapping process had to be the bait itself, the Sunny Jim that he'd learned to smear on a small plastic disc affixed to the cage's interior.

He'd tried pecan nuts the first day, which had attracted a squirrel that was savvy enough to grab the treasure and escape before the trap was sprung, but Daniel soon figured out that peanut butter couldn't be whisked away, forcing the squirrel to engage with the bait inside the trap.

Today's slightly mangy specimen sat on top of the rickety, wooden church fence, starving, desperate, a perfect exemplification of a life spent in the 'End.

Daniel watched it climb down the peeling fence post to the frozen ground, where it hemmed and hawed for a moment, taking stock of the situation.

The trap was a short wire cage with an end that would swing one-way only, allowing the animal ingress and access to the bait, but no escape, once fully inside.

Circling the cage warily, the rodent finally chanced it. It nudged open the wire door with its head, sliding inside on its belly as the door latched behind it, and it immediately went to town on the peanut butter, a de facto last meal for the squirrel before the squirrel would become a meal itself.

Daniel, wearing gloves, held the cage in front of his belly as he cautiously descended the basement stairs one by one. The squirrel was reacting much as the others had, chattering and furious at first (the gloves were a painful lesson learned) but now deathly still as they entered the darkness below, as if it could already sense its fate.

He stopped at the bottom step, waiting for his eyes to adjust to the light of the single, bare bulb. "Hey, I brought you-" His voice trailed off.

Nancy had been busy. In one corner of the basement was a pile of old books, papers, knick-knacks... all the contents of the crumbling boxes that had been stacked and stored down here over the last dozen years. Daniel's eyes picked out the yellow of several National Geographic covers in the pile, and a few hardcover volumes of Encyclopedia Britannica that she'd haphazardly tossed.

In the opposite corner of the basement, all of those now-empty boxes had been disassembled and put back together in a nightmarish, patchwork construction that seemed to be slathered with and held together by some kind of sticky, wet glue.

*She's building... what? A fort?*

The structure was disgusting and fascinating, its angles making no real sense to his eyes - the highest point reached to the ceiling, and the whole thing protruded from the wall a good five feet, with a single, child-sized entry hole at the floor.

The chain that was tethered to the basement support beam disappeared into that dark hole, but extending out of it were ten long fingers, Nancy's new fingers, mottled, chitinous and bristly. They withdrew into the hole as Daniel stepped softly onto the basement floor.

*Not a fort. A nest.*

He felt movement from the cage he was holding, a furious thumping, although the squirrel was immobile, frozen in place.

*That's his heartbeat. Pounding against the wire cage. He's terrified.*

*So am I.*

"Nancy?" he called out. "... what's going on here?"

He could see now that the entirety of the basement ceiling had hundreds, maybe thousands of gossamer strands hanging from it, swaying gently from an air current he could not feel.

From the small hole in the cardboard nest, movement: Nancy's fingers again, stretching out, laying lightly upon the basement floor, as if feeling for something, testing… the light? The air? Satisfied, they pulsed once and exited the hole like strange, five-legged insects that dragged her wrists and arms behind them.

Nancy crawled out of her nest, and Daniel had to stifle a scream.

She moved easily, quickly, turning her head to face Daniel, and he could see that her hairline had receded considerably, to make room for the second set of red-black eyes that had sprung from the welts he'd seen at her temples a few days earlier.

She'd jettisoned the filthy nightgown, completely comfortable with her naked flesh, the coloring of which now matched the mottling that had started with her fingers and face. Short, wiry hair sprouted from nearly every follicle, and as she twisted easily to stand, he saw two very angry red marks on both sides of her ribs, each about the size of a fist, and his brain started making connections that threatened to shatter his sanity.

She smiled, showing off a mouthful of needle-sharp teeth. "Welcome to my parlor, darling. How do you like what I've done with the place?"

Daniel shuddered at the sound of her voice, an octave lower now, and with a harmonized timbre that seemed impossible, the secret language of spiders, strained and forced through human vocal cords.

*Well… not completely human. Not anymore.*

"What have you brought me, my love?"

Daniel choked back a sob. "Oh, Nancy..."

"Shh. You've brought a gift. How romantic. Don't ruin the mood."

He fought the urge to run, to vomit. "Food," was all he could get out, presenting the cage and its occupant like a sacrifice to an ancient God. "Food. For you."

"That's very sweet, but..." Her eyes were dull, crimson, without pupils, and gave nothing away. "It's so small."

Daniel was unsure how to respond, and so he said nothing.

"It's very small," she said again. "And I'm so very *hungry.*"

The deep timbre of her voice had turned his bowels to ice water. "I can put the trap out again," he said, suddenly very conscious of the fear in his voice. "But it's winter. There's just so few..." he stammered a bit, took a deep breath and regained control of his thoughts. "The animals stay out of the cold."

Nancy tore her eyes from the squirrel, directed her gaze at Daniel. "Something else, then. Perhaps a box of free kittens at the supermarket."

He tried to keep his face neutral as his mind screamed in horror.

She smiled slyly at him, showing off her teeth again, as if she could read his thoughts. "We'll figure something out. For now, you can let him out of the cage."

Daniel felt a surge of relief. Perhaps this nightmare was coming to an end, despite what she had just asked of him. "You don't want him? Maybe-"

"I don't want him… in a cage. Just put it down and open it. When he's ready, he'll come out."

For a moment, he thought he could detect a bit of the old Nancy in her eyes, the Nancy that he'd first met so long ago, playful, sexual… hungry. It crushed him. His heart ached for simpler times. When she was still human.

He put the cage down on the bare concrete floor, then opened the wire door and stepped back, waiting.

The squirrel did not budge.

"You should probably just go upstairs, Daniel." Her voice was almost guttural, her eyes locked on the terrified rodent again.

Daniel nodded too quickly, and he nearly tripped over his own feet to get up the stairs. He forced himself to slow down as he approached the safety of the kitchen.

As he reached the top, Nancy called out to him, and her voice sounded almost normal: "Daniel? Thank you."

He glanced back down, grateful that the single, dusty lightbulb down there obscured more than it revealed. "What's happening, Nancy? What's happening to you?"

"Something beautiful," came her disembodied voice, nightmarish again. "I'm *changing.*"

"But… into what?"

From below, the squirrel began to chatter and then let out a high-pitched squeal.

Daniel shut the door.

# 5

Nancy was dreaming, or whatever passed for dreaming in this strange new world. Her thoughts were in English, and that happened less and less frequently, and almost exclusively while she slept.

In her dream she was floating in the water of Tillman's Depths, and reflected on its surface she could see the vastness of the universe, swirling gasses and space dust forming asteroids and planets and suns above her.

*It's the creation of the galaxy,* she thought, but she also understood that this was a phrase and concept her new

*spidermind*

brain would never compose. It just didn't work that way anymore. As the days passed, her waking thoughts seemed to revolve less around the worry and anxiety of her old world, her human world, and more and more around the movement and vibrations of the world that surrounded her. The immediate world. *Spiderworld.*

Sometimes she would feel the branches that occasionally scraped the bedroom window two floors above, like a discordant guitar note amplified through every pore of her skin. She knew where Daniel was at all times, could smell his anxiety as he fretted in the bathroom off the hallway or worried himself to sleep at night; felt his aura weaken and fray as he avoided the kitchen… unless he was bringing her food.

In her dream, comets and meteors spun and danced above her, trailing long, sputtering tails of fire. Occasionally, a comet would streak from the sky and collide with the planet, sending massive, painful shockwaves through her body.

She had given up trying to tame the hunger of her waking self - it could be reined in as easily as the physical transformation that was happening to her, which was to say, not at all.

Her skin, once so pale it was nearly translucent, was now dark and tough and chitinous, covered with thousands of stiff, wiry hairs that picked up every minute air current, noise, and attar in the world around her.

The transformation was painful. And somehow, not entirely unpleasant. This pain was different than the never-ending ache she had been consumed within for the last year. This pain, which she could feel through every bristly follicle, had a purpose, she thought. A destination.

A dream-current in Tillman's Depths spun her lazily across its surface, and she dunked her head under, eyes wide open, reveling in her brand-new prowess. She dove, kicking with powerful legs, with new, *extra* legs, eager to see what treasure might be discovered in these waters.

When she was awake, she found she could access her human mind well enough to speak, but more and more it seemed she was using it as a Rosetta Stone of sorts, in order to communicate clearly her thoughts to Daniel.

It was she who insisted they needed to keep the church operating at business-as-usual when he told her he was going to skip the service this weekend, maybe even close the church down.

*Why did I do that?*

She suggested it would actually bring more attention to their situation if he shut down the church for even one weekend.

But she knew that wasn't really the reason. The spidermind was seductive, aggressive. Overpowering, sometimes. It excited her and freed her, intensified her emotions. And it frightened her. Not in and of itself, of course. The spidermind was neither good nor bad. It simply *was*. But coupled with her emotional, human mind, it had become quite... devious.

She dove deeper and deeper in her dream, down through the darkness of the lake, past single-celled organisms that could only hope of adhering to one another someday; and then even deeper, into a primitive broth of water and methane, and hydrogen and ammonia, and there, *there*, at the center of the newly formed crater, she saw it.

A greenish, throbbing light, burning in the stygian darkness like a gargantuan, alien flare, a beacon that seemed to pulse in time with a groove she could feel more than hear, those familiar three beats, a triplet that was repeated over and over, filling her with awe and wonder and love and a phrase she knew as well as her own name, now:

"*Rho Natus.*"

She realized quite suddenly that she was not dreaming but remembering, and the irony of this was that she would not remember it when she woke.

Nancy opened her eyes, immediately alert, aware of the multiple vibrations that were crashing into her from the church and surrounding churchyard above.

The double doors of the church were opened, a deep rumbling that echoed through her hair and skin, and next to that, the relatively small echo she identified as Daniel, stressed and strained beyond his breaking point over the last few days.

And now, a new tremble, a shuffle of feet that she felt and instinctively recognized as one of the two or three regular homeless visitors, older men who allowed Daniel to sermonize to them for the reward of a doughnut and some coffee afterwards.

Her stomach rumbled angrily at the thought of food, a pain she had become used to and could not satisfy, certainly not with a rat or a squirrel.

She crept from her nest, dragging the heavy chain behind her, her hands and feet translating instant and limitless information directly into her brain. She could *feel* Daniel greeting each patron with a "hello," or a "thanks for coming," and she could see and smell the strain in his voice as an aurora borealis of shifting colors.

He was worried about her, of course. Worried about her metamorphosis. Worried that she might not be done with her transformation,

*i'm not*

worried that she'd be caught… that *he'd* be caught.

But she wasn't worried. Her brain didn't work like that anymore. *It is what it is.* Spidermind. Spiderthink. Spiderworld.

Finally, the church doors closed again and the eleven humans who had come to hear Daniel speak today quieted down, their movements feeling to her like soft fingers lightly strumming a harp.

Daniel stood at his podium, looking out at the small group of people who had shown up for service on this gray and dreary Sunday.

*What am I doing?* he wondered.

Jenny Thomas was there, of course, wearing another, equally distracting hat. Old Faithful. He couldn't remember the last Sunday she'd missed. And Old Man Morgret, who always surprised Daniel when he attended. Morgret & Sons Hardware was one of the few businesses that had hung in during The Great Kobbe's End Exodus many years back. Francois Morgret was actually the son of one of the original sons of Morgret and Sons, and the only remaining Morgret after his grandfather, father, and uncle had all passed away. Recently, he'd donated several of the tents that now occupied the vacant lot next to his store, earning the ire of many of the 'End's residents.

*Just what the hell do I think I'm doing?*

Daniel recognized a few other semi-regulars, including three of the vacant lot dwellers, who would always be asleep when the collection plate was passed around, but never failed to wake up in time for doughnuts and coffee after the service. He didn't mind, as long as they weren't visibly tweaking and bothering anyone else.

*You* all *deserve better than this.*

Near the back of the hall was Abel Helman, short in stature and temper, and next to him was a young woman in her mid-twenties that Daniel suddenly realized was Helman's daughter, Lauren. He hadn't seen her in at least ten years and was surprised to see her toting a child of her own, a girl who couldn't have been older than five.

*Time flies, even when you're not having fun.*

He squared his notebook and his bible on the lectern and cleared his throat. "Good morning. What a wonderful turnout."

Jenny smiled at him, and he wondered if she even understood he was making a joke. Old Man Morgret stared at him without emotion. The three vagrants settled in for a fifty-minute nap.

*Even you three deserve better than a minister preaching about faith when he has none himself.*

His knee throbbed painfully where Nancy had bitten him, and he realized he hadn't changed the bandage in days, he'd been so preoccupied with her condition. "How's everyone doing today?"

*I can't believe I'm doing this while my wife is transforming into some kind of monster below us.*

He took a deep breath and began to speak.

"Did you have a pleasant week? Got that raise you were hoping for? Picked up that new car you've been eyeing? Husband finally finished the remodel?"

He'd downloaded the sermon yesterday, after Nancy had convinced him that even the slightest hiccup in their schedule might bring unwelcome interest on the two of them, and now, reading these words, he realized how ridiculous they sounded.

He soldiered on. "Maybe it was an awful week, and you *didn't* get that raise. That old car gave up the ghost. Maybe your wife is climbing-"

*the walls, the WALLS, my wife is LITERALLY climbing the walls, BECAUSE SHE'S TURNING INTO A GIGANTIC FUCKING SPIDER*

He paused and cleared his throat. "Maybe your wife has you climbing the walls with all that bathroom remodel talk."

He had corrected himself, but his mind went blank for a moment, unable to recognize the markings all over his notepaper as actual words.

*I think I'm going to pass out*

He glanced up, heart pounding, his ears filling with a dull roar, and locked eyes with Jenny. She came every single Sunday for his words of wisdom. She tithed regularly and excessively. She was a good person and a good friend. *She deserved better than this.*

He clenched his hands tightly behind the lectern, digging crescent-shaped indentations into his palms. He smiled at Jenny. "Maybe your dog got sick. Ate all the rolls."

She chuckled, embarrassed but delighted to have been singled out. He watched the blush climb up her face.

Daniel felt his vision widening again, the colors in the room returning to normal. "Maybe your week has been cloudy, no sun in sight." He swept his gaze across the room, making eye contact with everyone but the three homeless men, who were already enjoying dreamland. "Seems like we can *all* relate to that. Snow for the last three weeks. No sun in sight for us, right?"

Old Man Morgret nodded and Helman and his daughter listened attentively, but Lauren's child was beginning to struggle in her mother's arms, restless and bored.

"Well," Daniel continued, "That's not entirely true."


Nancy cocked her head, zeroing in on a particular vibration fluttering through the wiry hair of her fingertips. She nudged the colors of Daniel's voice to the background, pushed past the tremors of light snoring coming from the homeless trio, past the general shuffling of feet and posterior that came naturally when sitting, and focused on the whisper of tiny feet, the struggle of a child trying to escape their mother's arms.

She smiled, a deadly crescent of jagged edges. She was famished, and there was a fly in her web.


Lauren Helman listened politely to the reverend's words but was distracted by the *bum buh-bum* rhythm of a migraine coming on, and she couldn't shake the feeling that something was wrong with the minister. It had been ten years since she'd last set foot in Kobbe's End, but Pastor Cook looked like he'd aged twenty. He seemed absolutely exhausted.

Kimmy, five years old and the source of Lauren's own exhaustion, began to fuss, kicking at the back of the pew in front of them, which was thankfully empty. Lauren put a hand on her daughter's legs to still them, and when that didn't work, she pulled the child onto her lap.

Lauren knew exhaustion when she saw it. She'd just moved back to the 'End after spending the last decade seventy miles away in Sunset, a town that she had to admit was also sputtering and slowly dying. It must be going around.

She'd come back after the sudden death of Kimmy's father in a grisly work-related accident. She and Adam hadn't been married, so his life insurance went unclaimed. Lauren's father was putting together the lawsuit (between grumbling about how she and Adam should have been married or why she never should have been with him in the first place), and she had moved back in an effort to keep what little savings they'd scraped together, originally earmarked for a home in Spokane, or perhaps Walla Walla, or maybe somewhere in Montana.

"When we face the storm clouds of life," the pastor was saying, "We need to be able to find the silver lining. We need to have something to hold on to, to hope for, to ground us, so that we do not end up being swept up by the storm."

The words connected with Lauren on a deeper level, a personal level, but Kimmy was struggling to escape her lap.

She hitched the child back up to a sitting position, but the five-year-old had gone boneless, slithering through her mother's grip and back to the church floor.

Lauren glanced over to see her father's disapproving glare, a look that she knew so well. It commanded, *do not embarrass me in public.*

"The storms of life can actually turn out to be a great opportunity, if we know how to look," the pastor continued, but now Lauren was sure that he was getting distracted by Kimmy as well. "This sounds a bit silly on the surface, I know. How in the world can this horrible experience also be a great opportunity?"

Lauren was keeping a hand on Kimmy's shoulder as the girl played on the floor, but even that was too much for Kimmy right now. She was trying to shrug the hand away, making a particular sound that every five-year-old instinctively knew, a whiny, staccato noise that could infuriate even the most patient of parents. But fighting a headache and the stress of her father's disapproval had worn Lauren's patience to record lows.

She grabbed the child's shoulders and straightened her so they were facing each other. Through clenched teeth she whispered, "You need to stop. *Right now.*" It was a gamble… The Clenched-Teeth Whisper might set the child right, or it might trigger a crying fit, and Lauren could see Kimmy's face starting to crumble and collapse, signaling an approaching tantrum.

Lauren's father stared straight ahead, his jaw tightening. There'd be words on the drive home.

In the front pew, she saw the woman with the ridiculous hat turn back to see what the fuss was, and Lauren responded with a narrow-eyed glare until the woman turned back around. *Mind your business, bitch.*

She let go of Kimmy before the tantrum could turn full F-5, whispering to the child, "Fine. Fine. Stay close. No running around. I mean it."

Nancy's eyes grew wide as the earthquake of the child's footsteps resonated against her fingers and exploded like multicolored paint bombs in her mind.

Her gaze shifted unerringly towards a corner of the basement ceiling, pinpointing exactly the location of the child on the floor above her.

Hand over foot, Nancy effortlessly scaled the cardboard-and-spit nest she had built, reaching the wooden beams above and adhering to the old ceiling as she crawled upside down along it, towards the pulsing light that was the child's life-force on the floor above.

The heavy chain connected to her collar pulled taut, and she stopped, annoyed. She brought one viciously transformed claw to the thick nylon around her neck and tore through it like paper, letting the chain drop heavily to the floor below her.

Nancy was gone. Only the Spider remained.

Lauren understood that people searched for reason and patterns to understand chaos and chance. She knew that linking coincidences led to superstition, and even believed that religion was just a publicly accepted form of such. But she couldn't shake the feeling that Reverend Cook had written this particular sermon for *her,* that a Higher Power may have nudged his hand to deliver a message to a woman the minister hadn't seen hide nor hair of since she was a teen.

"How can we find joy in trials?" he asked her, and Lauren's mind flashed to her dead boyfriend. "Who really wants to go through trials in life? I'll bet there's not many of us that want to experience hardship… but sometimes it's just part and parcel of this material world we all exist in."

So entranced by Daniel's words was she, and so distracted by his own trials and tribulations was Daniel, that neither of them noticed tiny Kimmy, bored and oblivious to everything as only a five-year-old can be, as she slipped through the church door that led to the Cook's townhouse.


Kimmy Helman was a typical five-year-old girl, no better or worse, and although she didn't quite understand that her daddy had died, she understood her daddy was *gone,* and that her mommy was very sad about it.

Kimmy was sad too. She missed her daddy, but she also lost her bedroom, and her preschool, and her best friend Bridgette, and Gwen and Benjamin and Veronica, too. So she understood what mommy was going through.

Still, having to sit through grown-up church where everyone had to listen to one person talking about things she didn't understand was a bridge too far, and she did not want to be there.

She hadn't expected the door at the back of the church to open so easily, but it had, and she wasn't going to waste the opportunity to go exploring in a new space.

A dark hallway greeted her. It smelled dry and dusty and was more than a little creepy. Daylight beckoned from one end of the hallway, and she headed in that direction.

The kitchen was older than the one she'd grown up with in Sunset, and not nearly as nice as peepaw's here in the 'End, where'd they'd been staying for the last several days. And like kitchens all over the world, every counter space was designed at a height to keep Kimmy from being able to see what was on them.

But she knew a refrigerator when she saw one, or *fridge*, as mommy called it, and she knew that they all contained her favorite thing in the whole wide world: food.

With a little effort, the 'fridge door unsealed, and she began to snoop. Its contents were sparse, unlike peepaw's fridge, which was stocked with 7-Ups and juice boxes and string cheese and fruit roll-ups. This church 'fridge had a funny, *old* smell, and held a gallon of milk, several bottles of water, and some apples and oranges that looked a little fuzzy on one side.

She grabbed an apple, biting into it and chewing loudly (she would have rather had a roll-up) as she let the 'fridge door close of its own volition.

She turned slowly, considering her surroundings, then stopped, swallowing the bite of apple as she took in the door with the broken lock. The door jamb was splintered and couldn't help but rouse her curiosity… and the door was open. Just a crack.

From the other side of that door, a woman spoke to her. A woman with a strange, deep voice.

*"Little girl..."* came the low, sing-song voice on the other side of the door. *"Little girl..."*

Kimmy's eyes widened, her interest piqued, and she reached up and placed the apple on the kitchen table as she took two cautious steps towards the basement door.

Daniel's leg throbbed and itched maddeningly as he spoke. He rubbed his knee back and forth against the edge of the lectern. It did no good.

He continued his sermon. "Since we know God has only good things in store for us," he said, knowing he was lying, "we can persevere because we know these trials are temporary. When we're in the middle of the storm, when the rain and troubles are pouring down, when the snow keeps falling and the problems keep piling up, it feels like it will never end. But it will. I promise you, it will."

Movement in the back pew caught his attention. It was Lauren Helman, he realized, apparently bored to tears, her head craning around, searching for anything more interesting than the bogus sermon he was delivering.

*I should just stop. I should stop and let these people get on with their day.*

Embarrassed, exhausted, he pushed on. "When we understand whatever issue we're dealing with is just a temporary blip within the Big Picture, then we can breathe. We can relax. We can even rejoice."

"Kimmy?"

Daniel glanced up at the voice, startled out of his own monotony, and saw his small congregation turn as one towards the back of the church.

Abel Helman sat stock-still, aggressively ignoring his daughter and everyone else's quizzical looks, tuned completely to Daniel as the blush on his cheeks spread to his forehead, but Lauren stood, looking for a hint of something between the pews.

The two Helmans were acting so radically different from one another that Daniel found himself on autopilot, attempting to decode the situation. But as it all became clearer, he faltered.

"Rejoice," he intoned. "It's a good word, isn't it? It literally means, 'Leap… for… joy…'"

And as he watched Lauren leave her aisle, Daniel snaked his hand into his front pocket, feeling for the skinny key that opened the privacy lock on the door at the back of the nave.

His pocket was empty, the key in his other pants, and he realized in his rush to ready the church for a sermon he was not prepared to deliver, he'd forgotten to lock the door to the living quarters.

And now there was a child missing.

"Ah, shit."

Kimmy crept deliberately towards that mysterious door with the broken frame. She was insanely curious, but there was a primitive part of her still-developing brain that knew *Fear of the Unknown*, and it was screaming right now, desperately trying to get through to her.

She stopped with a comfortably safe six feet between her and the basement door. She could see nothing but darkness through the slim crack that had opened, so she leaned forward and stood on her tiptoes, craning her neck to see better.

Still nothing.

She rocked back on her heels, her eyes taking in the full height of the splintered door jamb, and she finally decided against it. This door was just too creepy.

And that's when the basement door slowly swung open wide, revealing the top of a set of stairs that disappeared into darkness below.

Kimmy had begun backing away, eyes wide, when the woman's soothing/scary voice drifted from the doorway again.

*"Little girl… I have toys down here… I have dollies…and Barbies… and candy."*

Candy? The woman was finally speaking Kimmy's language. The girl halted her backward momentum, but couldn't stop the smile that was spreading on her face. "What kind of candy?"

When no answer came, she moved back towards the doorway, again stopping near the top of the steps and squinting into the impenetrable darkness below.

That primitive part of her brain was blaring klaxon alarms now, but Kimmy's love for candy was overpowering all else.

She took one step down, her hand reaching, reaching, searching for an unseen railing, and when she couldn't find it, it was already too late - she was off-balance, and about to tumble down those scary, hard, wooden steps to whatever lay below.

"Kimmy!"

And then there was a hand on the back of her shirt, caught up with a chunk of her hair and pulling on it hard enough to hurt, and she was swept back into the kitchen, her mother having yanked her from a certain fall and into a tight embrace that resulted in Kimmy bursting into immediate tears, more surprised than hurt.

Neither of them noticed the long, spidery fingers that curled from around the top of the door jamb and back into the darkness of the basement.

Daniel flew into the room and saw the open basement door first, his heart sinking like a stone.

But leaning against the kitchen table was Lauren, her daughter sobbing in her arms.

*Safe,* he thought, rushing to the basement door and slamming it shut. "Is she all right?" he asked, his back firm against the door.

Lauren nodded, lifting her chin away from Sara's head. "She's fine, she's fine."

"Thank God," Daniel said, and from the basement he thought he could hear heavy chain dragging against the concrete floor.

Daniel ended the service early, earning him three pissy looks from the homeless men who had endured his nasally drone without their coffee and doughnut reward.

The senior Helman apologized profusely for his granddaughter's actions, and Daniel tried to assure him that all was well that ended well.

To Lauren, who was still holding a slightly sniffling Kimmy, he said, "Thank you for coming, Lauren. It was nice to see you after so long. I'm so sorry about that little scare."

"It's okay," Lauren said. "Really. She's a master at getting into trouble."

Daniel smiled, appreciating her grace.

"You should probably get that door fixed, though," she continued. "In case something like this happens again."

"You're right, of course," he said. "Yes, I will."

Suddenly, Kimmy leaned away from her mother and pulled Daniel closer so she could give him a hug, and the minister felt a wave of emotion that threatened to bring tears.

Lauren watched with wide eyes. "Wow," she said. "She never does that."

"Then I will take it as a compliment," Daniel said, patting the little girl's back. "You be good to your mom."

"I will," was the child's reply, and then all three Helmans were down the church steps and making their way carefully across the slushy street, and Daniel felt a massive ache of longing and envy.

He turned to face the last straggler, Jenny Thomas and her ridiculous hat, of course.

"A bit of excitement today," she said.

He nodded and managed a tired smile. "I suppose so."

"It was a nice sermon," she said, the flowers on her hat bouncing just enough to be distracting. "Too often we forget to count the blessings in our life."

Daniel, who hadn't slept more than twelve hours over the last week and was definitely having a difficult time counting blessings, just nodded again. "True."

She put a hand on his arm. "You're doing a good job here, Daniel. I hope you know that."

Once again he was overwhelmed with emotion, tinged with guilt at how well he had fooled his friend. How well he had fooled them all, apparently. "Thank you," he said. "That's very kind of you to say."

"Nancy?"

He exhaled. "Not any better, I'm afraid. Still very sick. Not up for visitors at all." He locked eyes with the woman. "*At all.*"

Jenny looked almost comically pained. "Poor dear," she said. "You tell her I said hello, please? And I promise to bring by some brownies, soon."

Daniel shook his head vehemently. "Not necessary, please. She's just… having a tough time right now."

He could have sworn the older woman actually *clucked* as she shook her head. *Is she acting concerned? For me? Or has she always been this theatrical?* He honestly couldn't remember.

"Okay," Jenny said. "Get going and see to that beautiful little woman of yours."

"Thank you," he said. "I will. Right now."

Jenny Thomas stepped cautiously over a particularly evil and slippery looking patch of ice, eyes on the sidewalk. The last thing she needed was to slip and crack her skull wide open. Who would take care of Charlotte?

But as she sat in her Land Cruiser, heater on full blast, waiting for the windows to defog so she could leave the church's parking lot, she cast her memory back to the last time she had seen Nancy Cook in person.

September, it seemed to her, when the gravel on the side of the roads was covered in yellow, brittle grass, and the temperatures were still in the nineties. Three months since they had traded Netflix recommendations. Three months since they'd shared a visit over coffee and brownies, even though Nancy had not felt well enough to consume either. Three months, and now Daniel seemed very uncomfortable about Jenny coming by to visit.

She pushed the thought away, but it niggled at her as she pulled out of the parking lot and onto Main Street.

*Three months? That can't be right. Nancy started feeling sick in March, and-*

She slammed on her brakes, narrowly missing the sheriff cruiser as it rushed past.

*Not Wade*, she knew, remembering the many times he had stayed over, his vehicle parked in the driveway next to hers. *He drives that old Bronco. This was Walsh or Kay.*

Whomever it was didn't so much as glance her way as she skidded to a stop, and if she and Sheriff Chitwood hadn't had such an ugly breakup, she might have called the Sheriff's office and let them know what terrible drivers they had employed.

Instead, she looked carefully both ways and crept back out onto the street, her thoughts prior to her near-accident completely forgotten.

Daniel stumbled a bit on his way down the old basement stairs, catching himself by grabbing hold of one of the exposed two-by-fours along the wall to regain his balance.

He had a moment to imagine himself tumbling down the steps, perhaps breaking his neck in the fall, and lying paralyzed on the basement floor as Nancy slowly crept closer.

Shoving the thought aside, he made his way down at a safer pace, rubbing his sore hands on the black slacks that covered his throbbing leg. Everything seemed to hurt these days.

He noted the thick, sticky strands that crisscrossed throughout the basement now, the dozen-or-so carcasses of dead rodents that hung from the ceiling in tight cocoons.

*She's making her own webbing. But... how?*

A million horrific images crowded his mind, and he forced himself to focus on the thick chain that ran from the wooden beam in the center of the basement and disappeared into the spider hole of the damp nest she had constructed out of old cardboard.

"Nancy," he said, his voice strained. "Please tell me you had nothing to do with that."

There was no answer for several seconds, and he was about to speak again when Nancy broke the silence with her seductive and maddening voice.

"With what, my love?"

"This isn't a game, dammit!" he shouted. "If something happens here, people will find you! People will see you! The police will come!"

"If something... happens?" came Nancy's voice from the spider hole. "If what happens, Daniel?"

"If *anything* happens! If somebody... if somebody gets hurt."

The chain shifted, and a shadow passed in front of the spider hole.

"She came to the top of the stairs, Daniel. I had nothing to do with that. How could I?"

As if to punctuate her statement, Nancy rattled the chain again.

"And if she had come all the way down here," he said, "What then? Would you... would you have hurt her?"

Her soft chuckle raised the hair on the back of his neck. She hardly sounded like herself anymore.

"Hurt her? No, Daniel. I would not have 'hurt her'."

He let out a breath he hadn't realized he was holding, but then she spoke again.

"I'm very quick."

He could see the shadow of her filling the spider hole and realized she was coming out, both of her hands gripping the top edge of the nest entrance, followed by her face, terrifying and somehow more beautiful than ever in the dim light thrown by the single lightbulb.

And then a second set of hands came from within the nest, testing the air, feeling their way around the spider hole, dragging the rest of her body out, and Daniel felt his mind actually slip sideways a bit, a mind-quake, if you will, and he stumbled backwards, tripping on the bottom step and landing hard on his ass, crab-walking his way up the old stairs as quickly as he could.

"I'm hungry," Nancy said sullenly. "And you're starting to bother me."

Daniel made it up to the kitchen, eyes wide as he caught just a glimpse of his wife's new form at the bottom of the stairs.

"I suggest you don't come down here when I'm hungry," she called up to him. "Unless you're bringing me food."

ature of the redbacks
# part three:

# queen of the redbacks

*the secret language of spiders*

I

Daniel limped down the "Door Hardware" aisle of Morgret & Sons with a small shopping basket held in one hand. The store was mostly empty and Daniel was left to himself to peruse the various knob locks, deadbolts, and chain locks hanging from the wall display. He decided that a sliding loop lock would work best, something he could install high on the jamb and the door, out of reach of tiny hands.

He'd replayed the morning's events through his mind over the last several hours, but his imagination wouldn't let Kimmy come out unscathed. Instead, he kept seeing the little girl making her way down the basement stairs, where Nancy would then pounce upon her and drag her into that little spider's lair she'd created. Perhaps he'd have found only a single, discarded shoe…

Shaking his head to clear the thought, he dropped the loop lock in his basket. He snagged a Phillips screwdriver, a cheap hammer, and a box of 16-penny nails on his way to the check stand.

As he made his way to the cash register, past electric lawn mowers hanging on the walls and pallets of ice-melt stacked on the scarred linoleum floors, he rubbed absently at his throbbing knee.

He made a mental note to smear some antibiotic ointment on the bite and get a fresh bandage on it when he got home. The last thing he needed was an infection on top of everything else.

A new, horrific thought sprang to mind, gripping his amygdala tightly, and Daniel stopped dead in the center of the aisle.

*what if Nancy has somehow infected you with whatever is happening to her?*

Blackness crept in on the edge of his vision. He imagined staring into the bathroom mirror one morning and seeing the mottled skin, the angry, red marks that would signal the development of his new, spidery eyes, the twitching and fluttering of four new arms as they sprouted from his sides, four new arms with too many elbows, ending in hands with too many fingers and too many joints…

Squeezing his eyes shut, Daniel took deep, wheezing gulps of air until he could get a grip on his imagination.

He was sure the cashier would smell the crazy on his sweat, but she paid him no mind, either too old or just too distracted by the headache she was obviously nursing to care about whatever he was going through.

She rang the items up, placing them each in a thin plastic bag with the "M&S" logo printed on it. He pushed over some crumpled paper bills and she slid back some small, old coins and a receipt without ever making eye contact.

As Daniel turned to leave, he saw an end-cap display of a large, cardboard black widow hanging over several shelves of spray cans marked "Captain Zamora's Home Defender."

He stopped, his eyes drawn to the image of a cartoon hand (presumably the titular Captain's) holding a can of the insect killer and spraying it on several cartoon ants in military outfits with rifles and bayonets. The ants were in various stages of death; the leader clutching at his throat while his tongue protruded from between his mandibles, choking on the poison spray.

Daniel stood there for a moment, lost in thought and taking it all in, until his reverie was broken by the cashier's cigarette-weathered voice.

"You got an ant problem?"

He didn't look at her, just stared at the big, cardboard black widow. "Spider," he said.

"Eh," she said, noncommittally. "Works good on ants. Nothing seems to work on the spiders in Kobbe's End."

Daniel set to work as soon as he had stripped his hat, coat and boots off. Without a word to Nancy, he was hammering and screwing in the hardware for the loop lock, acutely aware that it must be agonizing for her and her new sensitivity.

He was consumed by a dreadful certainty that Nancy was no longer tethered to the basement's support beam, and every second he spent on the lock would bring her closer to barreling through the door and pinning him to their old kitchen table for one last meal together.

His fears were confirmed when he felt a soft bump against the other side of the door. The blood froze in his veins.

"Are you locking me in down here?" came her soft whisper. "That's not very nice. Not very *Christian* of you, if you get my drift."

Daniel marveled at the tone of her voice. He could hear Nancy within it still, but it reminded him of watching Rich Little on The Tonight Show many, many years ago. He was an amazing impersonator of celebrities, but every once in a while the impression would be off just enough to break the illusion. Daniel wondered who was impersonating Nancy right now.

He continued twisting in the last of the screws, fingers trembling as he slipped the bar into the loop as he did.

"Of course not," he said, his heartbeat hammering in his chest and ears. Could she hear that? He spoke as calmly as possible. "I just need to make sure nobody discovers you down here. That would ruin everything, wouldn't it?"

There was a moment of silence before she spoke again. "You're not planning on starving me out, are you, darling? Locking the door and waiting until I die, mad with hunger?"

Daniel turned the screwdriver with some effort, tightening the last of the screws. It didn't look pretty, crooked nails and splinters, gouges and scratches... but it looked sturdy.

He leaned his head against the doorframe, considering Nancy's words. Was he even capable of starving her out? Could he live with himself? Of course not. He was sure there was still much of the woman he loved on the other side of the door, despite her physical change.

"You know I would never do anything like that," he said. "In fact, I'll head out to find you dinner in just a few minutes."

From the other side of the door came a soft sliding sound and a light bump. Daniel imagined her testing its sturdiness, with two hands towards the top and two more hands somewhere in the middle and

*christ stop it you're going insane*

then two more near the bottom of the door, and then he heard the strange, soft rhythm of all of those nightmarish limbs as she turned around and crawled back down the stairs.

"Oh, good," he heard her say. "I'm absolutely starving down here. And please, no more squirrels." Her voice was drifting further away, and he knew she was squeezing into that horrific nest she'd created. "Cats would be fine," she continued, "If you brought a litter of them. Or a dog. The Perry's have that fat retriever…"

"Right," Daniel said, wishing she would stop talking, needing her to stop. "Right. I'll get the biggest thing I can find."

*God help me.*

He turned back to the kitchen door and slipped on his boots and jacket.

# 2

Snow was falling again as he trudged along Main Street. His feet crunched down the icy sidewalk, and he turned his face away from a middle-aged couple that was walking towards him. They acknowledged him by squeezing to one side, but they said nothing, ignoring the empty duffel bag he was carrying.

Dark clouds had socked Kobbe's End in and grew thicker as the sun set behind them, and Daniel could feel the temperature dropping with every second.

When he'd left, the wire cage in the church's backyard had been empty, the Sunny Jim frozen and untouched.

With dread in his heart, he'd gone hunting. The 'End had a large population of stray animals, and he thought he'd be able to find something fairly easily, but after an hour or so, he was no longer sure. And returning empty handed wasn't an option.

There had to be a stray mutt he could find, one he could provide some warmth and a last meal for. God, how had it come to this? His thoughts drifted back to Roscoe, the stray he and Nancy had adopted sixteen or seventeen years earlier.

Roscoe was a good boy, a smart dog that both Daniel and Nancy had loved like family. But when Roscoe fell sick in his old age, Daniel had vetoed Nancy's suggestion that it was time to put him down. He could see that the dog was sick, that his quality of life was waning, and when Roscoe finally passed away nearly a year later, Daniel carried a tremendous amount of guilt over making the poor dog live for so long.

And now Daniel was roaming the streets of Kobbe's End, looking for a stray that was big enough to satisfy Nancy's hunger. Could he have done this to Roscoe? Of course not. The thought was ridiculous.

He knew that keeping their dog alive too long had been out of selfishness. But he had loved him too much. He just hadn't been ready to let Roscoe go, no matter what kind of pain the dog was in.

And what about Nancy? He knew how much she worried about leaving him alone when she finally passed. More than once he felt she had willed herself to stay alive longer just so he wouldn't be left alone. And he could not deny his relief that she had.

*Is that love,* he wondered. *Or selfishness?* And if it was love, then maybe it was time to approach the situation with a new attitude. Was there a chance he could embrace this frightening journey Nancy was on?

The mewling of a cat somewhere nearby interrupted his thoughts, and he steeled his shoulders, focusing on the task at hand.

He followed the cat's cries to a residential alley and steeled himself for the task at hand. The alley had been ignored since the first snow had fallen a few weeks back, and he found himself fighting through twelve or more inches of snow in some places, difficult at the best of times, but ridiculously exhausting with his injured knee.

Above, the sky had gone full dark, and the town hushed, with only his footsteps crunching guiltily in the silent evening.

The cat turned out not to be in the alley, but in the fenced backyard of a small, dark house.

Daniel stared over the fence, searching the black windows for any sign of movement from within. From the back, it was impossible to tell if the house was even occupied. But the cat – a skinny tortoise shell – was on the back stoop, crying to be let in.

The house's windows stayed dark, the cat's pleas unanswered. Still, strays were one thing… he didn't relish the idea of stealing someone's pet. But Nancy was hungry, and the falling snow was definitely limiting this evening's options.

The wood and wire fence that surrounded the backyard was maybe four feet high, just a deterrent, not really tall enough to stop anyone who was intent on trespassing. Twelve feet beyond was the tiny concrete stoop upon which the cat tread back and forth. The snow covered slab was dotted with dozens of tiny paw prints.

Daniel limped over to the fence and reached his gloved hands beyond it, waggling his fingers to get the cat's attention and pursing his lips. "Pss, pss, pss," he said, and then again. "Pss, pss, pss. Here, kittykittykitty. C'mere."

The cat stopped its pacing, watching Daniel from the stoop, tail twitching erratically. Its posture said, quite clearly, "fuck off, weirdo."

Daniel studied the houses on either side. Their windows were dark as well. He tested the fence, gripping it with both hands and giving it a shake. It seemed sturdy enough. Using his forearm to clear several inches of snow from the top, he dropped the duffel lightly to the ground inside the yard.

Bracing his palms against the railing, he pushed himself up, counting on muscle memory to pull off a move that seemed so simple only thirty or forty years earlier. But instead of swinging a foot to the top of the rail to help pull up the rest of his body, his injured knee scraped painfully against the wire, and he landed hard against the rail with his sternum, trying two more times to hurl his leg over and finally succeeding in straddling the fence, chest heaving from the effort.

His entire leg throbbed, and he felt ridiculous. The cat continued to watch him closely from the tiny concrete stoop.

Grunting with exertion, he pulled his other leg up, then felt his balance suddenly shift and he fell, landing painfully on his back in the snow next to the duffel bag.

Wheezing, he turned and lifted his head in time to see the cat, who had clearly had enough of his bullshit, shake a small amount of snow from its fur and leap up and over the fence in one lithe motion, trotting without a care in the world down the snowy alleyway Daniel had just come from.

By the time Daniel had pulled himself to his feet, the cat was long gone, and he stood in the yard alone, the snow waltzing around him on a light but chilly breeze that had sprung up.

In 2001, Jenny Thomas, forty-one years old, found herself a widow. Her grief was a complicated emotion. She'd been with Phil for fourteen years, the last few of which had been an absolute nightmare. He'd been drinking more and more heavily to deal with the stress of his job, and they'd fought often and viciously, and he'd slapped her more than once in that last year, each time followed by a tsunami of guilt that resulted in him crying and begging her not to leave.

She had already formulated her escape plan and was just waiting for the right time to execute it when the Towers came down, taking Phil with them. It was a horrifying event of course, but one that greatly simplified her own life.

In 2007 she sold their little New York condo for a ridiculous sum of money (and not a moment too soon) and moved in with her elderly mother in the sleepy little burg of Kobbe's End. She'd arrived in the tiny town while it was still thriving and had been watching it die ever since.

When her mother had passed five years ago, Jenny had asked Daniel - the only religious authority in town - to officiate the funeral, and she'd been so happy with the service that she'd begun attending his regular Sunday sermon the very next weekend. She found that she enjoyed Serene Hope's non-denominational bent, and particularly Daniel's thoughtful approach to current social values.

She'd grown quite fond of the minister and his wife, the latter of which had, until a year or so ago, always helped with his church duties. When Nancy had fallen sick, Jenny had tripled her tithing, an action made easy by Phil's pension, her own savings, and the not-insignificant inheritance left to her by her mother.

But she could not deny that something had changed in Daniel Cook's demeanor in the last week or so. Her senses, sharpened by True Crime podcasts and Netflix, had made her sensitive to his unusual reactions to her offers of food and his obvious uncomfortableness whenever she mentioned she'd like to stop by. She hadn't been able to shake the ominous feeling that had come over her at the end of today's services, or the look of panic when Daniel had realized the little Helman girl was loose in the church's living space. He'd been worried, for sure, but why? Because the girl might have gotten hurt? Or was it something else?

Jenny was beginning to think that her friend, the pastor of Kobbe's End, had murdered his wife. And tonight she was starting her own investigation.

She didn't have a lot to go on. She'd considered reaching out to Francois Morgret or even Abel Helman, to ask if they'd had contact with Nancy more recently than she, but she already knew the answer. Daniel and Nancy were friendly and outgoing, but she had become their closest friend over the years, and if Jenny hadn't seen Nancy recently, then nobody had.

There was a part of her that didn't want to engage with Morgret or Helman, or *anyone* who was friends with Wade, if she were being honest. The break-up was still just a little too fresh.

She'd met the Kobbe County Sheriff at a fundraiser about a year back and they'd hit it off and started seeing each other, and nobody was more surprised than she was.

It helped that Wade was nothing like Phil. He was handsome in an "aw, shucks" kind of way and a genuinely good man, determined to serve and protect the residents of his jurisdiction.

But he was a man of a certain age, and she was a woman just a tad bit older than that, and neither of them had any patience for the others' bullshit. At the first sign of trouble, they had both bailed on the relationship.

There had been a couple of drunken nights afterwards that resulted in a week or two of awkward dating again, but each time ended uglier than the last, and she regretted deeply that there seemed no way to repair even a friendship now.

Jenny pulled her winter jacket over her ample shoulders and fastened each button as Charlotte danced wildly at her feet. The little dog knew a jacket meant a walk or a drive, both of which had been rare events while the town was snowbound, and Jenny felt bad at Charlotte's impending disappointment.

Part of Charlotte's interest could also be attributed to the large basket of freshly baked rolls that sat on the kitchen counter. The food, the jacket… it was all too much for her little doggy brain. She began hopping on her hind legs, whimpering with excitement.

"Charlotte, no," Jenny said. "Not for you. You know that."

Ostensibly, the rolls were for Daniel and Nancy, but Jenny had played and replayed in her mind the options of how the visit might go. She'd either show up at the Cook's back door and bullshit her way into the townhouse, where Daniel would hem and haw over how Nancy was much too sick to entertain visitors, or she'd get stopped stone cold at the back door. She figured either outcome would lend credence to her theory, which she would then present to the Sheriff's office and request that they perform a wellness check on Nancy.

*Or Daniel invites you in… and then kills you, too.*

The dark thought gave her pause, and the headache she'd been nursing on and off for days suddenly flared and pounded in her skull. She tried to ignore it. *It doesn't matter. I'll be on my guard. I know how to take care of myself. He won't be able to surprise me. And honestly... I can take him.*

Still, she opened a drawer and pulled out a pen and notepad. She'd bought it when she'd visited friends in Anacortes many years ago, but had found little use for leaving paper notes for herself, since.

But this note wasn't for herself.

*Wade,* she wrote at the top of the page, then immediately reconsidered and peeled that page out, crumpled it in her fist and dropped it in her wastebasket.

She started again.

"To whom it may concern," she said aloud, as she scribbled. "I have a very bad feeling about Nancy Cook and her husband, Daniel. If I'm missing, please check Serene Hope first."

She squared the notepad on the kitchen counter, then grabbed the basket of rolls and the keys for her Land Cruiser, eliciting another round of barking and dancing from Charlotte. Turning to the dog, she spoke in the sing-song voice of all pet owners, telling her to *be a good girl,* and *wish mama luck,* and *mama will be back soon,* and never once did she think she might be making a promise she could not keep.

Charlotte poked her head out of the swinging doggy door flap, watching her owner get in the SUV. She barked once as the vehicle slowly backed out of the snow-covered driveway and into the street, a small "yip" that could never truly convey the full spectrum of anxiety and frustration and betrayal she was feeling at being left behind. Then she turned the other way, peering into the darkness at the corner of the house.

Daniel stood there with his duffel bag, watching the Land Cruiser cruise down the street. He shifted his gaze back to the little dog.

"Hi, Charlotte," he whispered.

The dog hesitated for a moment, then left the safety of the doggy door, tail wagging furiously as she trotted towards Daniel.

Serene Hope leaped up in the Land Cruiser's headlights as Jenny pulled into the tiny, adjoining parking lot. Her heart was pounding in her chest and she took a moment to re-examine her theory.

Did she really think Daniel had murdered his wife? On the surface, it seemed impossible. He literally doted on Nancy every time she'd seen them together, and the consensus was he'd be lost without her.

But *something* was going on. He'd been acting very strangely, and Nancy hadn't been seen in the last couple of months.

She reminded herself that this was just a reconnaissance mission, to gather facts and information. She figured if she were actually let in to see Nancy, then no harm, no foul. But if she were stonewalled at the door, she'd reach out to Wade, no matter how uncomfortable. He'd understand.

Carrying the basket of rolls, she left the SUV and started around the side yard of the church, heading for the familiar back entrance to the townhouse's kitchen, passing two empty rodent traps on her way.

The windows looked dark. It wasn't late, but she knew the basic layout of the home. The living room didn't have any windows to show light or movement, and Daniel might be in there. Nancy would be upstairs, but no light escaped any of the second-floor windows, either.

Her heart pounded in her ears as she climbed the short concrete steps to the tiny stoop.

*You've got this.*

She knocked on the kitchen door. No answer. She knocked again, harder, but there was a stillness to the house that suggested no one was home.

*No one alive, anyway.*

Relief flooded through her, and she let out a deep breath. Her first instinct was to just leave, but then her thousands of hours of true crime binging took over.

*Try the door. See if it's unlocked. You'll never get the chance to check the house again. If Nancy's here, if she's that sick, she'll probably be asleep. You can leave without anyone knowing. Case closed, end of story.*

A thrill of excitement electrified her nerves, and she tried the doorknob. It twisted and unlatched. Straining to hear over her own heartbeat, she poked her head inside the door. "Hello?" She called out. "Daniel? Nancy?"

She hung at the doorway for a good thirty seconds before stepping in, gripping the handle of the basket of rolls in both hands.

Leaving the door open for a quick escape, Jenny stepped deeper into the kitchen, craning her neck around the darkened hallway corner, every sense on high alert.

There was an unnatural silence to the house, as if someone were waiting just beyond the shadows to leap out and attack her. Her imagination was going crazy, replaying the ending of every serial killer movie she'd ever seen, and she knew her senses could no longer be trusted. She had terrified herself.

Nerve completely lost, she slowly and silently backed her way through the kitchen towards the door again.

*this is stupid you're stupid what were you thinking if you get caught this is breaking and entering or trespassing at least*

From her right came a *thump,* and she nearly screamed. She jerked her head towards the sound, but there was nothing there - just a door to... The basement? She'd been in the kitchen many times before but never had occasion to ask about it.

*It came from behind that door.*

"Hello," she said, eyes wide as saucers. "Daniel? I know it's a little late, but I've brought some treats."

And from the other side of the door came a muffled reply. "Hello? Is that you, Jenny?"

*That's Nancy's voice, you silly nudnik! You were completely wrong!*

She let out a bark of relief. "Oh God, Nancy," she said. "I'm so glad to hear your..." She trailed off as she reached the door and saw the damage to it... and the very out-of-place lock near the top.

"Jenny," came Nancy's voice from the other side of the door. "Be a dear and unhook that lock, won't you?"

*He didn't murder her... he's locked her away!*

"Oh my God," Jenny said, dropping the basket of rolls on the kitchen table. "Did Daniel do this? Is he here right now? I'll go get the police!"

"No!" Nancy's reply was urgent and forceful. "No, he's not here. Hurry, unlock the door! I'm starving!"

*The pervert has her locked in the basement and he's starving her. Probably torturing her, too!*

Jenny was filled with an unbearable glee at what awaited her when she opened the door. A sex dungeon of some kind, she was sure. She steeled herself - Nancy must look a fright, malnourished, pale and weak from lack of sunlight, half mad from starvation.

Standing on tiptoes, she stretched her arm and unhooked the loop latch, swinging the door wide open.

"Nancy?" She squinted into the darkness beyond the stairs, telling herself to be strong for the minister's wife, but unable to hide the excitement she was feeling. This was every true crime follower's fantasy, stumbling upon a killer's lair and rescuing his latest victim!

She thought this just might be the greatest night of her life.

Daniel slipped on a patch of ice as he crossed the street to avoid the homeless camp coming up. He caught himself before he fell, wrenching his back painfully. The duffel bag looped across his chest thumped against his hip with a small "yip" from the dog that he'd wrestled into it.

He'd crossed a line tonight, he knew that. The guilt over dognapping poor Charlotte hung heavy on his heart, and not just at the thought of Nancy dining on the little Pom. Jenny would be heartbroken at the loss of her little family member, never knowing what had happened to her.

As far as Nancy's eating habits went, Daniel knew there would be no going back to squirrels after this.

*And what happens when a dog is no longer enough? What happens when she wants more? Do you really see yourself continuing down this path? Capturing larger and larger animals alive, somehow? You couldn't even catch a housecat.*

*It doesn't matter,* he thought as he caught sight of the church. Nancy was his light and his life. He would figure it out.

The image of little Kimmy at the open basement door sprang to mind again, and he was wracked with despairing anxiety. He thought he might be having a panic attack, maybe even a heart attack, and they'd find his dead body in the middle of the street, poor Charlotte trapped in the duffel he'd strapped to his chest. The sheriff would be called, and he'd definitely have questions. Chitwood would enter Serene Hope for answers, and then… and then…

He stopped, his stomach bottoming out as he took in the sight of Jenny Thomas's Land Cruiser parked in the church's tiny parking lot, a fine dusting of snow on top of it, except for the hood of the still-warm engine.

"Jenny!" Daniel burst through the wide open door of the kitchen, slipping on the linoleum floor and then regaining his balance. He dropped the duffel bag and Charlotte let out another yip from within.

Skidding to a stop in the middle of the kitchen, his mind quickly assembled the puzzle-pieces he saw scattered around him.

A basket of baked goods on the kitchen table. A single, still-wet rubber boot on the floor in front of the yawning basement door, daring him to come down, down, come down and see what his wife had done.

"Jenny," he called out again, but he knew he was being foolish. "No, no, no," he said, repeating the word like an incantation that could send him back in time, reverse this moment, take it all back and make everything better.

*There's still time to stop this. She only got here a few minutes ago.*

He slipped and skidded down the last few steps to the basement, landing hard again. His body was screaming at him from his tailbone, his back, his knee, his sternum. He brushed a thick gossamer strand away from his face, squinting in the dim light towards Nancy's nest.

It looked the same as he'd last seen it, a nightmare hodge-podge of cardboard and webbing, except now Jenny's single, bootless foot protruded from the tiny opening. The foot, covered in a wool sock with embroidered dancing monkeys, trembled violently as he watched, and then went still.

"God, no," he whispered. "Nancy… what have you done?"

"Get out, Daniel," Nancy said from within the hole. Her voice was even more distorted, perhaps because of the alien mouth that was forming the words, perhaps because that toothy mouth was busy feeding. "Get out now, or so help me, *you're next.*"

Biting his hand in horror and drawing blood, Daniel stumbled back up the basement steps and slammed the door behind him.

# 3

Daniel stood at Serene Hope's wide-open front doors, wearing his best gray suit and his thin, silver cross.

A line of people stood at the church's entrance, all waiting to come inside, and he greeted each one of them with a smile and a handshake as they passed him. He craned his neck out the door and peered down the street. The line of humanity seemed never-ending, as if the entire town had queued up to enter the church. He knew there was no way the small nave could accommodate the numbers.

But when he looked over his shoulder inside the church, the pews were empty. In fact, the line of people continued past the back pew and into the small door that led to the hallway and the rest of the living space.

The idea of this filled him with an icy dread, but he couldn't remember why.

He pushed his way through the line and squeezed through the door, breaking free into the kitchen, where his dread turned to stomach churning horror.

The line of townspeople continued through the basement door, and down those old wooden steps.

Crudely carved above the splintered door frame was a phrase Daniel did not recognize: "*Rho Natus.*" The sight of those words chilled him to the bone.

He started pushing and pulling his way through the queue, disrupting it violently, but the townsfolk put up no resistance and just shuffled back into place after he had passed.

Stopping at the top of the stairs, he stared down into nightmare.

Nancy had continued to grow, to molt and bloat, until it was just her eerily beautiful face, drenched with the blood of the townsfolk and fused to a great, black, hairy thorax full of multiple, twitching legs, and an impossibly huge abdomen that stretched and strained against all four walls of the basement.

The entire church was her nest now, and Daniel knew as she continued to devour the population of Kobbe's

End that the town itself would also become her nest, her gigantic, multi-jointed legs winding through the streets and avenues, hairy and chitinous, searching for more prey, for more food…

"Daniel."

His eyes popped open at the sound of her voice, the dream still fresh in his mind.

He'd staggered out of the kitchen and into the church, finally collapsing near his lectern, weeping openly as he'd stared up at the weird, abstract cross, weeping for Jenny Thomas, weeping for the loss, piece by piece, of his sanity, weeping for the horror that Nancy had become, and then the exhaustion had finally, mercifully taken him.

He didn't know how long he'd slept, but the church's windows were still dark.

"Daniel," came her voice again, soft and eerie,

*like a smile at midnight*

and he turned towards the door that led to the hallway. It was still open, but empty. Her voice had been closer than that.

Squinting into the corners of the church, he strained to find her in the shadows, then finally looked up to the church's high, vaulted ceiling, shrouded in darkness.

She was there in the highest corner, tucked into a tight, spidery ball, watching him intently. He could only make out her upside-down face at first, but then realized that what he had mistaken for deeper shadows behind her was actually the fat, bristly shape of what her body had become.

He wiped his mouth, shifting his eyes away from her before he could identify any more details. "You killed Jenny," he said.

"I didn't want to," she said from above. "I *had* to. She broke in, snooping around. Came down to the basement. She thought you had locked me away and threatened to go to the police."

Daniel leaned his head against the lectern, still refusing to look at her. "She was a person, Nancy. A human being. Not a cat, or a dog. A human. A *friend*."

"She was no friend," Nancy spat. "She snuck into our house. She saw what had happened to me and threatened to tell everyone. They would have come for me, Daniel. And then they would have come for you."

"I don't care," he said, and he meant it. "I don't care anymore. We need to stop this. We need to turn ourselves in. This is not who we are."

For a moment, there was only silence. Then:

"Of course. If that's what you want. Tell the police what happened. They'll only put you in prison. I won't be so lucky. They'll test me. Poke at me. Cut me open and see what makes me tick."

Daniel shook his head. "No. I'll explain everything to them. They'll figure it out. Come up with a cure."

He could feel her shifting position on the ceiling, but still kept his gaze on the floor.

"It doesn't matter," she said. "I'll kill myself before I'll let them take me. Is that what you want?"

For a moment, he considered sharing with her his recent thoughts of ending his own life, but he was shamed and weak and lost. "Of course not," he said, instead. "But this must stop. We can't go on like this."

"We don't have to," she replied, and her voice was seductive and sweet, harmonized and alien. "I can go back to animals. Even squirrels. This won't happen again."

He exhaled deeply, the shock and despair washing over him, crashing against the seawall of his mind. His hold on reality felt tenuous, and he wondered if a person could actually feel themselves going insane.

"I promise," she continued. "I swear to God."

Daniel laughed humorlessly, his eyes shifting unconsciously to the ridiculous art installation that dominated the room.

"But…"

He finally looked up at her, his eyes taking in all her awful glory. "But what?"

She smiled sweetly at him. "There's the matter of her car outside."

"Oh, God."

"You'll need to get rid of it," she said. "Tillman's Depths, I think."

He had a strange moment of déjà vu when she mentioned the lake. A brief image of the moon reflecting off that dark surface, and something more, but it was gone too quickly, and the more he reached for the memory, the more elusive it became.

He nodded and pulled himself to his feet. His knee, his entire body, screamed in protest.

"Oh… and Daniel?"

He looked up at her upside-down face, her many, many limbs tucked in tight, and remembered the way she had been gobbling up the residents of Kobbe's End in his dream.

"Leave the dog."

# 4

The surface of Tillman's Depths was so flat and smooth Daniel feared it might be frozen over, but that was not the case.

The Land Cruiser's headlights reflected off the falling snow and the lake's mirror surface as he pulled up to shore from the old logging road, and he quickly shut them off for fear of being noticed from one of the few homes with an illuminated porch light on the other side of the lake.

It plunged the surrounding area into an eerie black and white of shadow and snow, and he jumped when Charlotte leaped from the back into the passenger seat next to him. She let out an anxious whine.

"I know," he said, petting the dog, attempting to calm his own nerves. "You miss your home."

*And your mama, but there's nothing I can do about that, now.*

He'd scooped up the duffel bag-full of dog as he'd left the church to dispose of Jenny's vehicle. Against Nancy's direct wishes, he'd decided to take the dog back to its home. It was a minor victory for Daniel, but he felt like he'd recaptured the faintest shred of his humanity, and Nancy owed him that much.

The Land Cruiser had handled the snow like a dream, and there was a moment sitting at one of the four stoplights Kobbe's End boasted, that he thought about turning the vehicle around and hustling Nancy into the SUV and spiriting them both away tonight, perhaps finding some place in Idaho or Montana to hole up, or maybe the Olympic National Forest, just find a small cabin in the woods where Nancy would be safe.

Where his town would be safe from Nancy.

But then what? Keep her hidden away as he taught himself to lure game back to the cabin? Or maybe just let her roam the forest herself, finding her own food and fattening herself up on raccoons, deer... hunters.

He'd pushed the thought away, feeling the lure of Tillman's Depths, a physical feeling that pulsed in time to the painful throbbing of his knee. He'd driven to the deserted end of the lake on the old logging road this time, a known make-out spot thirty years earlier, but now just an overgrown and unkempt area where the water met the shore at a gradual incline.

More than one car had accidentally rolled into the lake here when a parking brake was knocked undone by a bare, sweaty, teenage leg. Palmerton's Towing had a special "Tillman's Depths Fee" many years back, but the town's teenagers, few that they were, were too involved with phone screens to frequent the lake anymore.

Daniel opened the door and Charlotte leaped out into the snow, immediately searching for an appropriate area to relieve herself.

With the door chime ringing repeatedly, Daniel shifted the SUV into drive and got out as quickly as he could, fearful that he'd slip and get run over as the Land Cruiser bobbled down the incline and into the black water.

There was a moment of sheer terror when it looked as if the vehicle was going to stall while it was only half-submerged, but then the front end dropped steeply and the back end bobbed up, the interior lights shorting out and going dark as the whole vehicle sank in a flurry of bubbles.

Daniel felt a sudden longing to follow the vehicle down, down into the dark waters that both Decraine Kobbe and Richard Tillman had disappeared into more than a hundred years earlier, never to be seen again. Was this what Nancy was feeling when he pulled her out and away from the lake only a few weeks earlier?

*I should have let her go down, he thought. Should have grabbed her hand like I did, but let her take me with her, instead. Wherever she was going.*

The bubbles finally stopped, and the night grew so still that he could hear the snow falling and gathering on the limbs of the surrounding trees.

Charlotte trotted up to him, watching the lake where the vehicle had disappeared into it. She barked once.

"Let's get you back home," he said.

Jenny Thomas's home was less than two miles from Tillman's Depths, but by the time Daniel had stumbled out of the thick tree line that surrounded the lake, he was already exhausted, his quad muscles burning. Each breath he took threatened to start a coughing fit or perhaps mercifully freeze his lungs solid.

He could see that Charlotte was struggling as well, and the little dog put up no resistance when he finally bent over and scooped her up, carrying her even as his back wailed mightily with the effort.

Daniel appreciated the silence that enveloped him, the momentary peace and quiet, but as he trudged down the middle of a road bordered on both sides by black woods, he was overcome with a profound sense of loneliness. For the last twenty years, Nancy had been his rock. He shared everything with her. There had been no problem they hadn't been able to solve together.

*Except,* he thought, *she was the problem now.* And she was unwilling to deal with what was happening to her. She seemed to relish the changes her body was undergoing. She'd killed Jenny.

*Eaten her.*

Daniel felt uniquely alone in a world that was spinning increasingly out of control, with no one to turn to, no one he could ask for help or even advice without endangering Nancy. Who could possibly understand this kind of situation?

The ground glittered and crunched beneath Daniel's feet and the road ahead was flat enough that he could see the glow of downtown's streetlights, even a mile or more away, a beacon that drew him onward, through the black hole of towering trees that flanked both sides of the road.

He heard movement in the woods to his right, and he struggled to drag his eyes away from the hypnotic ideomotion of his own feet, one in front of the other, over and over again as they trudged towards town.

The warmth of Charlotte pressed against his arms and chest, and he noted that the little dog made no movement even as the crashing from the woods drew closer, louder.

Daniel's head finally cooperated, and he glanced towards the sound, seeing movement beyond the trees, a silhouette of something blacker than black in there, wispy and surefooted and now slowing to keep pace with him.

*A wolf,* he thought, then pushed it aside. *No. Too big. A bear?* And there was a weird comfort in the thought. Facing off against a bear in the snow was far from appealing, but he figured he wouldn't survive the encounter, and there was a grim relief that his journey might end this way. It didn't sound nearly as bad as it might have just a few months earlier, and it was certainly more mercy than he deserved.

But the movement in the woods was too thoughtful, too precise for a bear, and as Daniel squinted into the darkness, he saw that the silhouette of the creature was too thin in places, too rigid, too mechanical in its motions.

And then he finally put it together, made sense of the figure in the shadows, and he could pick out its joints, its elbows and knees, if you will, of which there were far, far too many; and its furry plumpness, its shape too round to be a dog, or a wolf, or a bear, or a mammal of any kind.

The glow of the snow reflected in its many eyes. It turned towards him, crashing through the underbrush and bursting onto the road next to him, a monstrous spider the size of a Volkswagon, grabbing hold of him and shaking and squeezing and biting and he only realized he had been dozing when he was awakened finally by Charlotte wriggling furiously in his arms.

He dropped the dog, and she ran excitedly through the snow to the front gate of her own yard, barking and hopping up and down, beseeching Daniel to flip the gate latch open.

He did so, his arms heavy and aching, wondering at how he'd sleepwalked from the lake to Jenny's house, and for a moment all he wanted was to follow Charlotte as she raced across the yard and through the doggy door into the warmth of her home.

But he knew the morning was fast approaching, and even if Jenny had left her door unlocked, he dared not leave any more evidence of himself at her home, so he closed the gate and latched it, and began trudging towards the church.

When Charlotte burst back out of the doggy door, having completed a yipping lap through her house and finding it confusingly empty, Daniel did not notice.

The bass-drum combo intro to Golden Earring's "Radar Love" kicked in, and Deputy Walsh cranked the volume on the Crown Vic's stereo as he cruised just a little too fast down SH 200. It was already past four in the morning, the highway was empty, and he was itching to get to Tillman's Depths before sunrise and the end of his shift. The heartbeat of the lake throbbed louder and clearer the closer he got to it.

He barreled down the lone exit ramp for Kobbe's End and took the corner of Colby and 4th at nearly thirty miles per hour, feeling the cruiser's snow tires slip and the Ford's rear end fishtail a bit before finding traction.

*Just like Bullitt,* he thought, Marlboro dangling from between his lips, fingers drumming against the steering wheel in time to the song's wave in the air.

"We don't need a letter at all," Walsh sang softly, finally slowing as he entered the town proper.

The 'End didn't have its own radio station, but you could get the classic rock station out of Heather if you didn't mind your Def Leppard tinged with a little static, and on a clear night you could grab the Erik Zann Midnight Metal Hour on 105.7 all the way out of Yakima.

Walsh cruised through residential Kobbe's End, tapping the brakes again, bring himself within fifteen miles per hour of the posted speed zone. The roads were completely empty tonight, partly because of the weather, partly because of how late it was, but mostly just because the 'End was a struggling town on failing life support.

So when he rolled into downtown and saw the silhouette of the figure trudging along the snowy sidewalk, he felt a surge of excitement, assuming it must be one of the tweakers from the canvas city next to the hardware store.

Some nights, Walsh would pull up across from the lot full of tents, eyes narrowing as he studied the filth and crime and despair on display.

If someone were to toss a Molotov cocktail in the middle of all that nylon and canvas, he thought, it would go up like a powder keg.

A deputy could look forward to a hefty raise and a nice promotion if he were to rescue the unfortunate souls caught in a conflagration of that type. Conversely, that deputy might look forward to a much lighter workload if he were to turn a blind eye to it.

The clock read 4:26 AM as Walsh turned the stereo off, and he rolled his shoulders and neck with a satisfyingly loud crack, flicking his smoke out the window. He sensed an "aggravated assault/felony resisting arrest" charge coming on.

Imagine his surprise and disappointment when he lit up the Appleton and its searing white light revealed the pastor of Kobbe's End, Daniel Cook.


Daniel was on the verge of collapsing, and he knew if he stumbled, he wouldn't have the strength to even lift his hands to break his fall. He was entertaining the thought of just lying down in the snow and taking a short nap when he was suddenly lit in bright light, and the blue and red flashers began to strobe almost directly behind him.

His head whipped up as if he'd been given a shot of adrenaline directly in the heart, and as the deputy's cruiser slowed down and stopped next to him, he plastered a smile on his face that he hoped didn't look too insane. He wasn't sure how they'd found Jenny's sunken SUV so quickly, but he instantly realized that his tracks in the snow would lead directly from him to the far shore of Tillman's Depths.

The passenger window of the cruiser rolled down and Deputy Walsh leaned over his steering wheel to get a better look at Daniel.

"Christ almighty," Walsh said, "that you, Father? What are you doing out this time of night?"

Daniel's mind raced. He hadn't been found out, it seemed, but now he needed a story. He shrugged almost comically, as if to say, *oh, you know me!*

"I had to take care of Mrs. Thomas," he blurted, immediately horrified with himself. "Her dog, I mean. She's sick again. Charlotte, that is. Jenny is completely fine and healthy, actually."

*shut up shut up stop talking SHUT UP*

Walsh rolled his eyes and groaned, clearly not a fan of the woman. "Jesus. That fucking dog." He glanced up, suddenly aware. 'Scuse my language, Father."

"Oh, it's just 'pastor', Deputy. Or Daniel. Daniel's fine."

"You got it."

Without warning, the passenger door unlocked loudly, and Daniel tried not to show the panic he was suddenly gripped in.

"Hop in," Walsh said. "I'll give you a ride back to the church."

"Oh, no," Daniel said cheerfully. "I'm fine. I actually enjoy the exercise. Really."

"Bullshit," Walsh said, and his voice was commanding. "It's on my way. Get in the car. You're completely soaked."

Daniel contemplated making a break for it, almost laughed at the thought. He nodded and opened the door, pulling himself into the cruiser.

The Crown Vic's windshield began to fog up as soon as the door was closed, and Walsh flipped the defroster on full blast. Daniel couldn't help but appreciate the warmth that flooded the cab. His face began to tingle, pins and needles as his skin attempted to adjust to the sudden temperature change. His back ached from the cold and abuse heaped upon it all day, and he made a conscious effort to hide the pain and stiffness from the deputy to avoid conversation. The fewer questions, the better.

As if on cue, the deputy spoke. "You're a hell of a friend. What's wrong this time?"

Daniel looked over at him, a deer in the headlights. "I'm sorry?"

Walsh glanced at his passenger. His own eyes seemed quite sharp. "With Champagne. The dog."

"Charlotte," Daniel said automatically. "She, uh… she got very sick. Ate something she shouldn't have. Again."

Walsh chewed on his lower lip, digesting the information. "Isn't that more of a job for a veterinarian? Why would she call you all the way over in the middle of the night?"

Now the deputy was looking straight ahead, concentrating on the road, but Daniel felt as if his own thoughts had been laid bare, x-rayed and transmitted directly into Walsh's brain.

"That seems a little weird to me," the deputy finished, and the interior of the Crown Vic was suddenly crowding in on Daniel.

"Sure," he said slowly, rising to the occasion. "Only vet is in Heather, though. Jenny knows how early I get up, took a chance on calling. I answered."

Walsh said nothing for a while, and Daniel's brain played out scenario after scenario as the deputy chaperoned him through the silent, snowy streets of Kobbe's End, each storyline ending with Daniel fleeing the cruiser once it stopped, and then being gunned down by the deputy. A vengeful Nancy would explode out of the church's front doors, quickly dispatching and dismembering Walsh as Daniel's vision began to blur, darken, and finally fade to black…

They pulled up in front of Serene Hope, and Daniel, ready to bolt, glanced guiltily at the deputy. Walsh looked distracted, uninterested in his passenger.

"Do you hear that?" Walsh said, softly.

"No," Daniel said.

Walsh, who seemed almost in a trance, snapped back to reality and smiled at the minister. "Well," he said, all teeth, "It's still pretty early. I hope you can get a couple more hours of sleep, at least."

Daniel watched the man's eyes, searching for… what? Would the deputy mention this encounter to Chitwood? Daniel knew Jenny and Wade's breakup was ugly. Was there any reason to think the sheriff would reach out and discover she was missing? Would it lead back to Nancy? Daniel unlatched his door. "Me too," he said, and slid out of the vehicle. Before closing the door he leaned back in. "Thank you. I appreciated the warmth."

"No problem, Pastor," Walsh said. "Get back to your wife. She's probably worried sick."

Daniel closed the door and Walsh immediately pulled back into the snowy street and drove away.

*Oh…* Daniel thought, *I doubt that.*

He closed the kitchen door against the weather and unzipped his winter jacket. It was soaked through and weighed a ton. The wet coat fell to the floor as he kicked off his boots and trudged lifelessly through the kitchen, past the basket of rolls on the table and the open basement door, and then up the stairs to the second floor.

In the darkness of the bedroom, he stripped off his clothes, peeling his drenched underwear and socks from his ice-cold skin and falling into bed, pulling the covers over him. He began to shiver uncontrollably, reflexively twisting his body into a fetal position until he finally lost consciousness.

Under the bed, darkness. A still, primeval darkness that had frightened man since the dawn of time.

And in that darkness under the bed, something darker. Something *blacker*, something *weighty*.

Nancy's spidery fingers fluttered against the bottom of the bedspring, tantalized and tempted by the shivering, living body above her.

Walsh studied Tillman House as the cold light of the rising sun began to illuminate its blackened ruins. In the darkness, the charred corpse of the old mansion was full of shadows, maybe even ghosts. Secrets, definitely. But as the sun crawled across the frosty ground, it revealed the burned and rotting timbers as only that, the remains of a house the history of which had been romanticized exponentially over the years.

He followed weeks' worth of his footprints in the snow past the ruins to the lake, standing at the icy shore and staring across its steaming, unfathomable depths.

It sang its song to him loudly and clearly, a message that he had memorized but did not yet understand, a triplet that was now accompanied by words sung by an inhuman choir in a language he did not recognize.

Just being within close proximity of the lake seemed to energize him and sharpen his senses, his ability to focus.

He'd come to the Depths with no real purpose this morning, just a need to be closer. As was often the case, the clutter in his mind was swept away, replaced with focus and clarity.

The urge to visit the lake had been strong back at the church, strong enough to distract him from the cagey way the pastor had been acting, but the more the deputy thought about it, the more strangely it sat with him.

Jenny Thomas was an insufferable bitch, that was common knowledge. She was loud and abrasive, and Walsh had been hired on when her relationship with the Sheriff was in its last spasms. He'd witnessed some of her nutty bullshit up close and personal.

But she loved her dog. More than anything.

If there was an honest to goodness pet emergency at four in the morning, would she call the preacher instead of the veterinarian? She and Cook were friends, yes. But still… the story was fishy.

The pastor himself was fishy, and Walsh thought there was much more to the little man than he let on. But was it worth investigating?

He bent down and picked up a flat rock the size of a silver dollar and skipped it across the lake's glassy surface, daring the water - or the God within - to speak to him, to reveal its secrets.

The lake responded as it always had, in a throbbing beat Walsh could feel, but a language he did not know:

"*Rho Natus.*"

The gray morning light through the bedroom window crawled slowly across the floor, and then over the bed that afternoon, and finally faded away against the far wall that evening. Daniel's body barely moved that entire time, and if he dreamed, he mercifully could not remember them. When he opened his eyes it was dark again, and he stared up at the ceiling as he stretched his body, acutely aware of his overworked back, his injured knee, his aching calves.

"You've slept the day away," Nancy said.

Her voice came from beneath the bed and his heart sank, overweighted with guilt and despair. It suddenly occurred to him that he had reached out to God, had begged him for guidance and help, and yet every time it had been offered to him he had rejected it and pushed it away, whether it was Jenny Thomas, Michael and his doctor friend, or even Deputy Walsh last night.

He shifted his gaze to the darkness outside the window. "So I have." He sat up, robotic, emotionless.

"It's dinner time." Her voice was a terrifying whisper.

Standing up and shuffling to the bathroom, he could hear Nancy following behind, pulling herself from underneath the bed first, followed by the soft padding of the tips of her multiple limbs, a maddening rhythm, a *scuttling*, if you will, that started on the hardwood floor and then easily, horrifyingly, moved to the ceiling.

Daniel refused to look, turned on the cold water in the bathroom sink and splashed his face with it. He reached for a hand towel to dry off, staring at his sickly visage in the bathroom's oxidized mirror.

A flicker of movement in the reflection behind him caught his eye, a slender, hairy, multi-jointed arm shyly curling up into the darkness of the hallway ceiling beyond the door, as if embarrassed to be caught in the light.

Looking away quickly, he combed his wet fingers through his hair.

From the hallway came Nancy's voice, almost playful, as if they were in the middle of some bizarre game of hide-and-seek, in which she was determined to be seen and he was equally as determined to avoid seeing her.

"Squirrel will be fine tonight," she said, as if ordering off a menu. "But I'll need more than just one. A small dog would be better."

Daniel ignored the implication but thought of poor Charlotte and how he'd left her alone last night. He'd have to swing by and make sure she was fed while he was out this evening.

He shut the light and left the bathroom, catching just a glimpse of a shadow down the stairwell in front of him, and then he followed it into the kitchen.

Daniel's jacket was still damp, but he paid no mind, grimly fastening each button. Behind him, Nancy crawled the ceiling, the old building shifting and creaking occasionally under the unfamiliar weight of her new form. He kept his gaze on the floor.

"Don't be too long," Nancy said from somewhere above him. "I need to keep myself healthy, you know."

He gave no indication that he heard her as he opened the kitchen door to face the night again. The cold breeze caressed his face.

But before he closed the door, he leaned back in and pulled a set of two tarnished keys from the old wooden key hanger above the light switch.

# 5

The soft giggles and bass beat coming from the tent next to his own was really starting to piss Nikos off.

Earlier, he'd run into Matt and Diane, the older, hippy dippy occupants of said tent, and they'd claimed to be in possession of a fair amount of Ecstacy. In fact, they assured him it was pure MDMA, and the music and giggles next door certainly seemed to prove that out.

But whatever they'd sold him - a light blue tablet with a Tesla logo pressed into it - was not having the same effect on Nikos. His jaw was aching from clenching it so tightly and he felt sweaty and nauseous, on edge. His headache, a near constant triple beat for the last three days, was now threatening to crack his skull wide open.

Fentanyl was always a possibility, but he'd had it before and knew the effects. This felt more like the pill had

*the secret language of spiders*

been stepped on with meth maybe, or even baby laxative, the way his stomach was gurgling, and he was sure that Matt and Diane had purposely sold him bad drugs.

The giggling next door increased in volume, and his needle redlined. He opened his mouth to scream at them to shut the fuck up when he felt his insides twist and his brow suddenly bead with sweat.

He was going to shit his drawers.

"Fuck," he whispered, clenching his ass cheeks tight enough to crack walnuts. He crawled out of his sleeping bag and carefully slid into his pants, begging his stomach and bowels to obey his commands for just a few minutes longer.

He ducked out of the tent and paused, groaning as another series of cramps ripped through his stomach.

Matt and Diane moaned in delight from the tent next to him. *Fucking assholes.*

He made his way through the lot's pathways with short, quick steps, pulling his jacket on and heading towards Hoyt Ave, the gutter of which had been unofficially agreed upon as the public toilet for the residents of the canvas city.

In the freezing weather, you could almost ignore the smell of the daily feces of a hundred humans, a fact that Nikos was grateful for as he hurriedly unbuckled his pants and dropped them around his ankles just in time for his bowels to empty in a steaming liquid stream into the gutter.

In the summer heat though, Hoyt Ave had become unbearable, and so nobody but the homeless had been there for the last two years. The businesses on either side of the street - a couple of lawyers' offices and the old Kobbe's

End Cinema - had shuttered their doors in spring of 2020 and had never re-opened.

Nikos had worked for Mister Lai at the cinema during the summer the year before the pandemic hit. Nikos liked Lai. He was a good guy, treated his employees well, and really knew his movie trivia.

That summer had been ridiculously hot - as they all were in Kobbe's End - and the theater had done great business. Even if the movies being shown sucked, people would go anywhere that had good AC.

There had been an incident during a matinee that August. A little girl was bitten by a spider. Commonplace in the 'End, but the bite proved to be from a Black Widow, and Lai had closed down the theater for a few days so that he and Nikos could fumigate the joint.

They'd found an infestation of Black Widows in a closet that hadn't been opened in years. "Redbacks," Lai had called them. He'd placed a spider de-fogger in the small closet and set it off, shutting the door and sealing it at the bottom with a towel.

"I don't mind spiders," Lai had told Nikos. "You can't be bothered by spiders and live in the 'End. But the Redbacks and the Recluses gotta be killed as soon as you find them. Too dangerous for the little kids."

Nikos shivered in the cold, looking up at the marquee of the cinema. "Underwater", the big black letters spelled out, and he thought that sounded about right, until he was distracted again by the relentless clenching of his bowels.

*Pure MDMA my ass.*

He lamented losing the smack he'd bought from Rahner a couple weeks back. That guy always had quality product.

But it was really the Sheriff's fault that Nikos had no drugs, that he was hanging his bare ass out in the freezing weather over a street gutter filled with shit.

*Fucking Chitwood.*

It was Chitwood's bust that had kicked off Nikos's streak of bad luck this time. First he'd dropped his smack, then he'd been humiliated by his old sunday school teacher.

*I should have kicked Cook's ass that night and taken his money and his booze,* he thought, pulling a crumpled newspaper page from his jacket pocket. He clumsily and painfully wiped his ass with it.

Next time he saw the old pastor, he was going to do just that. Take the money and slap the living shit out of him for daring to embarrass Nikos.

He pulled up his pants and stood there for a few minutes, making sure his stomach wouldn't betray him again.

*The next time you see him could be tonight,* he thought, *if you really wanted. You know where he lives.*

Jeffrey Walsh watched the pastor pull out of the church parking lot in a car that the deputy knew wouldn't pass roadworthy requirements on the best day of summer, much less in this icy weather.

Walsh had burned through half a pack of smokes as he waited in the darkness across the street all evening, watching the church from the warmth of his own car, a ten year old Camry that he'd purchased with his Kobbe County Sheriff Department signing bonus. He hadn't wanted Cook to see a department vehicle across the street.

Walsh had left Tillman's Depths this morning and went back to the station to clock out, then home, where he tried unsuccessfully to nap. He'd finally come back to the church for an unofficial stakeout as soon as the sun had set, waiting, waiting... but for what?

*Rho Natus,* apparently. Whatever the hell that meant.

He watched the taillights of the pastor's death trap wink out of sight around a corner, heading in the opposite direction of downtown.

Whatever Daniel Cook's business, it wasn't in Kobbe's End.

He pondered this for a moment, his foot tapping unconsciously along with the comforting triplet that was his constant companion. Should he follow the minister?

*You know, this would be a perfect time to take a peek in those old church windows,* he thought, grabbing his Mag Lite. *See what's got the minister acting so jumpy.*

Walsh grasped his door handle, then froze, eyes on the figure that had suddenly appeared from behind his Camry and was now creeping across the snowy road towards the back yard of the church.

*Well, what do we have here?*


Nancy had watched Daniel take the old keys and now felt a rumbling vibration through every pore on her body, one her human mind identified as the Chrysler she and Daniel had been gifted last year. That alarmed her for the briefest moment - *where was Daniel going? why did he need the car? was he ever coming back?* - but as the vehicle vibrated out of the range of her senses, the Spider assumed control again, and she was suddenly and completely obsessed only with her hunger. Instincts were taking hold, instincts older than man, perhaps older than Earth.

And now a different instinct took control as new vibrations flowed towards her from the farthest reaches of her web. Something was approaching the church.

Some*one*.

Pastor Michael Davis refilled both glasses with five fingers of scotch this time, placing one on the wood table in front of the couch Daniel Cook was sitting on. He sat down in his old easy chair, facing his friend, and took a long pull from his own drink.

"Okay," he said. "I'm still a little fuzzy on why you've driven all the way up here in this weather…"

Earlier that evening, he'd just sat down with a cocktail and an episode of *December* when the motion lights in the driveway had come on, illuminating an old red Chrysler that Michael recognized as Daniel and Nancy's.

A stab of guilt hit him at whatever could impel Daniel to drive from Kobbe's End to Heather in a car that looked as if it would not survive the return trip. He'd felt bad for the way he'd ambushed Daniel with Peter Rawlik, and had been meaning to call and apologize, but his own church duties had taken up his time this week and he'd never gotten the chance.

Inviting him in, Michael had offered a drink to calm Daniel's obviously frayed nerves. And then, sitting in his den, he'd listened to his friend of twenty-five years spin a tale of lost faith and a dying wife and love that knew no bounds, but had clearly been taken advantage of.

Daniel glanced up at Michael over the rim of his glass with bright eyes before taking another sip of the scotch. Michael was surprised his friend had accepted the offer of a second drink, but watching him consume it was equally unexpected.

"Guidance," Daniel finally said. "I need your wisdom, Michael. I seem to have reached a point in my life where I am in need of counsel and discretion."

Michael studied his friend. The man looked exhausted beyond words, maybe even caught in the fever of illness, but not... crazy. Still, there was a fervor in his eyes that made Michael uncomfortable, something he couldn't quite nail down.

"Have you ever had to do something horrible," Daniel said softly, "something that went completely against your morals even, but you knew you *had* to do it?" He glanced up and briefly met Michael's eyes, then looked away. "Maybe even... *hurt* somebody? And there was simply no other choice?"

Michael's eyes narrowed, suspicious of the suddenly generic question. "The Bible certainly has plenty of instances of-"

"No, no, no," Daniel cut him off, scowling. He took another gulp from his glass. "Not 'The Bible'. I'm not interested in parables tonight." He drunkenly unfurled one of his fingers from the glass and pointed it directly at Michael. "You. Have *you* ever had to do that?"

A hateful memory occurred to Michael, a memory of coming home from middle school and finding that his dog Tilly, a mutt of exceptional character, had been struck by a car, but not killed outright.

Michael had cradled the bloody dog in his lap, crying for nearly an hour as she stared up at him with confused, agonized eyes, unable to move but refusing to die.

Finally, Michael's father - a no-nonsense commercial fisherman that Michael had only come to appreciate after he himself had become an adult - had handed his twelve-year-old son his hunting rifle with the words, "Michael, tend to your dog."

He'd hated his father that day, who had always called him "Mikey-bones" until then, and hated Tilly too, if he were being honest, for not having the good sense to die after the truck had spilled most of her guts along the busy county highway they lived next to. Hated everyone in the town, in the state, on the planet that day. Hated God, too. But he had tended to his dog. And he suddenly knew what Daniel was asking him.

"Yes," he said carefully, sipping lightly from his own glass. "I've had to do that."

He studied his friend, expecting Daniel to elaborate, but the small man only nodded, throwing back the last of his glass and moving on as if he hadn't heard.

"Did you know that scientists believe they've only identified about twenty percent of the world's spiders?" He looked up with a manic smile. "The things you research when your wife is dying."

"Is Nancy…" Michael paused, unsure how to phrase his question, fearful that Daniel had already committed the deed. He started over. "Is Nancy okay?"

Daniel chuckled, attempted to slurp another few drops from his empty glass. His eyes met Michael's again, and this time they did seem crazy. "'Okay'?" he asked, nearly cackling. "She's more than 'okay', Michael. She's strong as an ox! You should visit sometime! Why, you wouldn't even recognize her!"

Michael let out a sigh of relief. *Still alive then,* he thought. *For now.*

Nikos quickly made his way to the fenced backyard of the church, eager to be out of the open. He'd watched the minister leave in his rusting hulk of a car, but had no idea how long Cook would be gone, and he was already losing his nerve. Being a generic piece of shit was easy, he'd discovered. But he wasn't accustomed to actual breaking and entering.

He tried the back door first, his much-preferred point of entry, but it was locked tight. There was something about using a door - regardless of trespassing or the like - that felt somehow less illegal to Nikos.

The kitchen window had a length of wood dowel in its gutter, preventing it from opening, even if it hadn't been secured.

But the small window down the side of the townhouse slid when he pressed his palms against it, and he opened it quickly, hoisting himself up and inside with one fluid movement that Daniel would have been very envious of.

Nancy waited in the darkest shadows of the church's vaulted ceiling, silent, patient, feeling and hearing the clumsy movements of the boy outside as he inspected the entrances.

He'd found the window she'd unlocked, opening it slowly and silently. It felt like a freight train rattling by at full volume. As he slipped inside, she uncoiled her body, nearly pulsing with excitement.

Nikos crouched, waiting for his eyes to adjust, his ears attuned to the slightest sound.

After a moment, he relaxed. No one had heard him. The house felt empty to him, but he knew that Mrs. Cook was sick, dying, even. So she was most likely sleeping. Hopefully wacked out on painkillers.

*She'll be sharing those tonight.*

He was in a tiny bathroom. *Makes sense,* he thought. Bathroom windows are opened and closed constantly. *Easy to forget to lock it back up. Nobody likes the smell of shit.*

He closed the window as silently as possible. *They should try Hoyt Ave once in a while. It might put things in perspective.*

He rifled quietly through the drawers under the bathroom sink, finding no drugs, but stuffing two rolls of toilet paper in the big pockets of his jacket. If he could avoid wiping his ass with newspaper for the foreseeable future, then this stressful little excursion had already paid off.

From the bathroom, a cramped, dark hallway led to the left and the right, and he snuck towards the stairwell to the left that led upstairs.

*The bedrooms. That's where the drugs will be. In a nightstand or a vanity.*

He'd have to be quiet.


Outside, Walsh licked his lips, his heartbeat flipping and skipping in time with that of Tillman's Depths. He opened the Camry's glovebox and pulled out his Beretta APX, his off-duty weapon, a comfy 9mm that he loved and was looking forward to using on that junkie Nikos.

He figured the kid would be in and out of the church quick, so he exited the Toyota and closed the door as silently as possible.

The flurries continued, catching in his hair as he followed Nikos's footprints through the snow. They lead along the side of the church to a gated backyard.

Walsh positioned himself inside the yard, scanning the fresh set of footprints to the back door of the adjoining townhouse, and then along the back of the building where they ended underneath a small window. Based on the window's size, Walsh guessed it was a bathroom.

*The punk will come out the same window,* he thought, *and probably bolt as soon as he sees me.* He figured he'd have to shoot as soon as Nikos hit the frozen ground.

*Suspect ignored my repeated commands to stop. Suspect charged violently. I feared for my safety.*

Walsh was getting hard just thinking about it.

Nikos stopped at the top of the stairs, his senses on high alert for movement, for presence.

The silence of the church was unnerving. He felt like one of the battle-hardened soldiers in those old war movies his grandpa had liked. "It's quiet," they would always say. "*Too* quiet."

But it was too quiet. Houses made sounds, it was a fact. Sometimes from settling, or sometimes from the wind outside, but mostly just from the people living in them.

*Snoring,* he thought. *The old woman's bedridden. Why can't I hear her snoring? Or clearing her throat, if she were awake. Or a television, or music, the turn of a book page,* anyfuckingthing *that sounded like someone else was in the house.*

The silence was getting to him and he could feel his resolve crumbling. He needed to shit or get off the pot. *Looks like this is a night for shitting.*

As he crept towards the bedroom door, he passed another small bathroom. Movement within nearly elicited a shriek until he realized it was his reflection in the mirror over the sink.

Chastising himself, he continued to the open bedroom door, leaning his head inside and squinting towards the bed.

The old woman lay dead there, her eyes wide open but unseeing, staring at the ceiling. Her mouth hung open, her hands crossed over her chest. By the worst stroke of luck, he'd broken in on the night she'd finally croaked, and now his DNA was scattered all over the place.

But, no.

The bed was empty.

Nikos stared, confused, chewing at the inside of his cheek. Had he worked himself up this whole time for nothing? Maybe the wife had been in the car when the minister left? He cursed himself for not paying closer attention.

But then another thought sprung up, curdling his blood. He felt his bowels clench again.

*Maybe she's still in the house.*

Had she heard him and hidden herself away? Or worse, was she armed and creeping around the dark space that she was completely familiar with, watching his every stumbling move and waiting for her chance to attack?

The thought raised goose flesh, and he shook it violently away. He took three angry steps towards the bed, peering over the far side, and then dropped to his knees to look under it. The old woman wasn't there.

*Empty. The place is empty. This is the best possible option. Get what you can and get out.*

Next to the bed was a small nightstand, and atop it sat the mother lode: a half dozen tiny, orange pill bottles with white caps.

He scooped them up, holding them close and squinting at their labels before jamming them all in his pockets.

*Vicodin,* excellent. *Percocet,* also excellent. *Opana,* he wasn't familiar with, but that had never stopped him from having a good time. And then, the big winner: *Kadian.*

*Morphine,* he thought, with a thrill. *Thank you, Jesus.*

He cringed at his own thought. Nikos wasn't a big believer in God and the afterlife, and certainly not The Devil. But if there was a Hell, he thought that breaking into a church and stealing an old lady's prescription medications while making fun of Jesus was probably a sure-fire way to end up there.

He moved swiftly down the stairs now, uninterested in being quiet or hiding his tracks, determined to just get while the getting was good.

There was no need to tumble back out the window he'd entered, so Nikos headed for the kitchen and the back door that had denied him entrance.

In front of him, he could see the glow of the winter landscape seeping through the window over the sink, but he stopped, eyeing the dark shape of the refrigerator. He was pushing his luck, sure, but why not load up on some food while he was here? There sure as hell wasn't anything else of worth in this dump.

The light from the open refrigerator cast long, dark shadows throughout the kitchen, but it wasn't until he had nearly closed the fridge door, annoyed at the minister for the lack of food available to pilfer, that Nikos noticed the clutter surrounding him.

Leaving the door open for illumination, a twinge of anxiety settled uncomfortably upon him. Nikos lived in filth, yes, but he knew that most others did not, and there was something wrong with this kitchen.

The floor was stained, somehow slippery *and* sticky, untouched by broom or mop for what must have been weeks. The sink held a number of dirty dishes, chunks of dried food caked to their surfaces. The room smelled like vomit, and made his own bile rise in his throat.

And then there was the black, splintered doorway he finally noticed behind him, open wide and strangely inviting, but the refrigerator bulb was intimidated, too weak to illuminate the darkness beyond.

Nikos took a step towards the doorway, drawn against his will by its dark mysteries, his mind racing, calculating, unable to quantify the information he was receiving.

*What's going on here?*

The church seemed as if it had been abandoned in the middle of the night. If he hadn't watched the minister leave earlier, Nikos wouldn't have believed anyone had been here in weeks.

He reached the basement door, staring down a wooden staircase that disappeared into wispy, inky blackness.

There was a pressure in his bladder, in his stomach, his chest. Peering into that yawning void petrified him, paralyzed him, rooted his legs to the kitchen's tile floor.

And an odor now, a scent, a *niff* wafting up from the basement, the smell of death, yes, but old, dry death; cloying, sweet.

His mouth went dry, and he could taste the fear on his breath, sharp and tangy. He was going to vomit, he was going to shit himself, perhaps both. He had taken the Lord's name in vain while he was robbing a church, and now he *did* believe in The Devil, and he also believed The Devil was there in that blackness under the church, and if he didn't tear his eyes away, if he didn't get his legs moving, if he didn't *RUN AWAY RIGHT FUCKING NOW*, that basement Devil was going to come rushing up those stairs and drag him back down to Hell with it.

He took a tentative step back from the threshold, a high, soft keening involuntarily escaping his lips. He was terrified, yes, but felt a surge of relief at regaining control of his limbs, that he was getting out of the church, getting away from whatever lurked in that dark basement.

But he was wrong, he realized, finally catching a glimpse of the monstrous shape on the ceiling above him, the refrigerator light glittering in those eight, dull, red eyes.

The Devil wasn't in the basement anymore.

Walsh watched the darkness of the bathroom window intently, sure that Nikos would be climbing from it at any minute. He held the APX easily, loosely, finger resting outside the trigger guard, anticipating his first human kill.

*Finally.*

When the shriek came from within the church, he was immediately energized. Had Nikos surprised the old woman? If the kid had hurt her, nobody would care if Walsh gunned him down afterwards.

His thoughts were interrupted almost immediately by the back kitchen door exploding open, Nikos leaping down the steps to the ground and running full throttle towards the deputy, as if hell were on his heels.

"Freeze," Walsh shouted, raising the gun, finger sliding over the trigger. It was strictly theatrical. If there were any witnesses, better safe than sorry.

But then from behind Nikos, a dark shape filled the kitchen doorway, a set of giant, chitinous, *spidery* hands gripping either side of the doorframe, followed by another nightmarish set near the top of the door, pulling, launching out into the night the mottled, spiky torso and bloated abdomen of a gigantic spider, easily the size of a human. And atop it all, the head and strangely familiar face of a beautiful woman.

*Holy shit,* Walsh thought. *Is that Nancy Cook?*

*Run, little human, run.*

Nancy's senses lit up like a Christmas tree at the burglar's scream, the smell of his fear broadcasting at 50,000 watts. She shifted unconsciously into *Spiderthink* as the boy scrambled away, the pounding of his heart washing over her, electrifying her brain and every wiry hair on her body.

He hit the back door hard, unlatching and wrenching it open in a surprisingly fluid motion, and Nancy exploded into action, her limbs moving her effortlessly across the ceiling to the floor and then to the doorway as the thief slipped and stumbled down the outside steps.

She paused for a half a second as the freezing air hit her skin, the outside world transmitting itself to her through one limb that now touched the cold, hard ground of the backyard. Thousands and thousands of colors, scents and sounds crashed over her.

The air carried the vibrations of the drifting snowflakes and the mass of humanity in the tent city only a few blocks away, the scent of a fake log burning in a fireplace somewhere beyond Kobbe's End, and especially the throbbing beacon that called to her from the darkest depths of the lake near the center of town.

All of that information washed over her in the blink of an eye, all of that and something else: there were *two* humans trespassing in her backyard.

Near the gate, another stranger stood, radiating shock and surprise and gun oil and arousal.

*Not him,* she instinctively decided, not yet, and she pushed all of the information she was drowning in aside in the blink of an eye, focusing instead on the terrified boy that had broken into her home and was attempting to escape.

*Him.*

She was on top of Nikos in an instant, her limbs forcing him into the snow, smashing his face and bloodying his lip against the frozen ground.

He cried out in pain and terror and Nancy moaned in ecstasy, gripping his arm and opposite leg with two of her limbs and lifting him above her, struggling and screaming, as she reared back upon the rest of her many legs.

She flexed - *and it was just a tiny flex* - and Nikos exploded in her grip, blood and gore showering over her, pill bottles flying through the air, his torso falling to the ground, steaming in the freezing air, twitching as he gasped again and again. Still holding a dismembered arm and leg, she turned to face the other intruder.

The man's features triggered something in her human mind, a memory from a lifetime ago - a face at Williford's Market perhaps, or maybe the county fair in Heather - and Nancy hesitated, her own face and chest splattered with Nikos. She dropped the torn and dripping appendages that were cooling in her grasp, squaring herself to leap at the man near the back gate.

He surprised her.

Slowly and carefully the man knelt in front of her, his hands outstretched. He placed his gun softly on the snowy ground.

His eyes met hers, and the awe on his face, the *love*, the absolute *devotion*, made it clear that he was not surrendering. No, definitely not surrendering.

This was adoration.

This was reverence.

This was *piety*.

"I… I…" the man stammered, then squeaked, "I live for you."

Nancy cocked her head, studying him, feeling his arousal, his *lust*, roll over her in waves. It wasn't unpleasant.

"I live to *serve* you," he said, his voice stronger.

Nancy reached down and slowly clutched Nikos's bloody, dead body from the ground in front of her. She scooped up each torn limb in her other hands.

She then backed herself carefully up the steps she had recklessly charged down earlier, leaving a trail of pink, trampled snow. She dragged Nikos with her, his head bumping audibly against each step to the kitchen door. The boy's eyes were still wide open, frozen in terror. The snow that fell from the pitch-black sky settled upon them and refused to melt.

Before she dragged the corpse down into the basement, Nancy craned her neck to peek back into the yard, considering the man outside again. He was still posed in genuflection.

*Interesting.*

Michael watched Daniel's eyes close for several seconds before they slowly opened again and attempted to focus on him.

His friend was clearly exhausted, and on his fourth scotch - a feat that, before tonight, he would have swore was impossible - but he also looked... what? Relieved, maybe? Unburdened.

Daniel's eyes regained focus and he caught Michael studying him.

"I'm at a loss," Michael said. "Tell me how I can help you. And Nancy, of course."

Daniel smiled sadly up at him. "I'm not asking for help. I guess... I guess I'm asking for forgiveness."

"There's nothing to forgive, tonight." *I hope.* "A good night's sleep is in order. We can discuss this with fresh minds in the morning."

He stood to help Daniel to his feet, but the smaller man resisted.

"No, no," Daniel slurred. "I can't stay here. I don't know what she might do if I'm not there. She might get out."

That last sentence gave Michael pause. "You're in no condition to drive, Daniel. I can't believe that old death trap even made it here in the first place. You're staying tonight. In the morning, we'll both go back to the 'End. We'll get this sorted out together."

He watched Daniel's eyes lose focus again, and rather than try to navigate his intoxicated friend through the house to the spare room, he decided to bring a blanket and pillow out to him on the couch.

Daniel was already dozing when Michael returned with the cover, but as he spread it over him, the drunk man spoke:

"I think maybe she's right."

Michael waited for more, and when it didn't come, he gently said, "Right about what? What do you mean?"

"That this is supposed to be happening," Daniel said, slurring his way through the sibilants. "That this is God's will."

Michael said nothing, but his mind went back to what Daniel had said earlier. *I don't know what she might do if I'm not there. She might get out.*

"I still love her," Daniel slurred, and then immediately started snoring.

Michael grabbed both of the scotch tumblers, downing the last of his in one gulp as he ferried them to the kitchen sink. While he was rinsing them, he came to a conclusion and wiped his hands dry on a dishcloth.

He pulled out his cell phone, bringing the screen close to his eyes as he thumbed through his contact list, stopping and pressing the 'call' button on the name *Peter Rawlik*.

Rawlik was a bit of an odd duck, yes, but Michael knew him as a good man, a smart man, a *discreet* man, and perfect for the job he had in mind. He expected to leave a message this late at night, but Peter answered the phone immediately.

"Peter," Michael said quietly, craning his neck to make sure Daniel was still asleep on the couch. "Sorry to be calling so late, but I've had a rather odd visit from Daniel Cook. I think something horrible might have happened in Kobbe's End."

There was silence on the other end of the line, but finally Peter spoke. "What do you mean? How can I help?"

"Well," Michael said, "I need a welfare check on Serene Hope. Depending on what you find, we may need to involve the police. I think Daniel may be thinking of helping his wife kill herself."

There was another stretch of silence, and Michael didn't know whether to curse his cell signal or if Rawlik was debating the favor.

"Of course," Rawlik finally said. "I'll head over there right now."

# interlude:

# the testament of Decraine Kobbe

*the secret language of spiders*

TILLMAN IS DEAD, the fiend, and I, his murderer. I held his head underwater and watched him sink to the bottom of the lake that bears his name.

Understand, my regret is only that I had not wrapped my hands around his devilish throat a year past, or four years, when we first founded Kobbe's End together, or twenty years before that, on the day he saved my right leg and left hand - and perhaps my life - at The Second Battle of Murfreesboro, when I was but one of a thousand wounded soldiers, and he one of too few field medics.

In my pain and delirium that New Year's Day, looking at the ruin of my leg, femur shattered by Confederate (or, just as likely, Union) minnie, I'm sure I promised a great many things to the devil with the bone saw in his hands. But something in my pleas must have resonated with Richard Tillman, for he set to work on my *extremities with a fervor, and though I've walked with a limp ever since, I've needed no extra support in the passing decades. My hand, though not pretty, still functioned well enough to strangle the man.*

*Would that he had amputated, or treated with less care in order for infection to take me. How many lives might have been saved had I not fallen into his debt and under his wicked spell?*

*BY THE END of the war I had been promoted to Colonel and was pursuing a political career in Pennsylvania when I crossed paths with Tillman again.*

*His skill as a surgeon had taken him far, and meeting each other again at the Governor's mansion was a welcome surprise that afforded us an opportunity to introduce our wives.*

*Katie, my sweetheart since grade school and my wife upon my return to Williamsport, was thrilled to meet the man who had saved her husband many years earlier.*

*Of Eva Tillman I shall write very little, for her gruesome fate is still fresh in my head, and I do not understand much of last night's catastrophe.*

*But that night many years back, I remember being surprised and more than a little jealous, for she was strikingly beautiful, though perhaps a bit too young for the doctor, and very gregarious, a trait that she shared with Katie. The four of us became fast friends.*

*the secret language of spiders*

The Tillmans were new to Williamsport, and while Richard established his practice, Katie took much of her time to introduce Eva to the community and the city. They were nearly inseparable.

As for myself, I had been recently elected to the Pennsylvania House of Representatives, with my eye set on a seat in Congress.

In those days, I shared more than a sip of whiskey with Tillman, and I learned that besides his obvious brilliance in the medical field, the man had a vast knowledge and curiosity of esoteric religions and spiritualism.

These were risky interests - some might even say blasphemous - but although I have claimed Christianity as my own religion, my time as a soldier and a politician have eradicated any belief of a benevolent God I may have had, and the events of last night have cemented that.

Had I known how deep his interests in the occult lay, how dark his own belief system ran, I would have cut all ties immediately, and perhaps my little Christina and the rest might still be alive today.

Tillman had lived in Seattle for a scant year before enlisting in the army, and many of our whiskey-soaked evenings consisted of him regaling me with tales of the beauty and untapped opportunity of the Pacific Northwest, the availability of land, and the population explosion expected when the Northern Railroad was finished.

*He had dreams and ambitions of founding a community, a town, and he would catch me up in his fervor, exciting me with the idea of adventure and a legacy left to our children. He and Eva spoke often of a large family, and my little Sarah was already one and one-half years old.*

*WHEN MY BID for Congress failed, the Tillmans were there to console me, our planned celebration devolving into a commiseration party, instead.*

*But when President Hayes afforded me an appointment to the Department of the Interior in '79, Tillman was guiding my hand and my wishes, and I was granted my request as special agent for Oregon, Washington and Idaho.*

*The five of us headed West, and four long weeks of train and wagon had us settled in the Yakima Valley, where Tillman and I surveyed and platted our nearly 4.5 square miles of legacy around a pristine lake surrounded by forest and field. I feared confrontation with the natives, called the Senjextee, but saw not one during our original survey expedition, and have heard of only peaceful encounters since, which have fallen few and far between.*

*The natives' indifference towards the land and settlers around the lake seems far more ominous to me now. Surely the Senjextee are aware that there is an evil stain upon Kobbe's End. Its origin must be many hundreds of years old.*

*Tillman proved an excellent surveyor, far exceeding my own knowledge and experience, but I realize now I should have been less impressed and more suspicious of the natural landmarks that seemed to spring up exactly where the devil needed a turn or a corner.*

*Damn my foolishness, for even then it seemed as if someone had traversed these hills and woods before us, and I know now that it must have been Tillman himself, drawn to this cursed area some years before he convinced me to join him on his hellish journey.*

*Damn my foolishness, and damn my vanity, because I knew something was awry when Tillman produced a plat map of our proposed town shortly thereafter - much too shortly thereafter - but my suspicions were assuaged by the town's name lettered beautifully at the top of the map.*

*"Kobbe's End," he'd said, and the flattery smothered the suspicious thoughts that were kindling in my mind.*

*Tillman's Depths, read the words overlaying the body of water in the middle of the map, and I hope whatever calls those depths its home is feasting on his water-logged corpse right now.*

*WE SOLD THOSE plots immediately, going into summer of '81 with a population of sixty-one people who were proud to call Kobbe's End their home. The community was strong, neighbors becoming friends, and all* of them - including Tillman and I - pitched in with homesteading and tree clearing when needed. Although our gardens and crops were troubled by aphids, mosquitos, beetles and wasps, we persevered.

Sixty-one people, no matter how courteous, required a Constable, and Walter Johnson was elected. He was a fair and honest man who saved my life last night, even as his own was taken by that devil, Tillman.

John Fulton, a salty, old, retired miner who opened our first saloon, believed that the ground of Kobbe's End had minerals worth exploiting, and would tell anyone who would listen at the watering hole that he had enough dynamite to get started on a mine. Constable Johnson and Fulton had a disagreement about the greasy sticks of explosives that Fulton was storing in his saloon, and I am reminded today that those dynamite sticks now reside in the Constable's back storage barn.

OUR TOWN SEEMED to blossom, with the population growing to over 400 by spring of '84. Katie and I had done our part, introducing our beautiful Christina Lee Kobbe to the town a year earlier. Sarah, almost six then, was extremely proud of her little sister.

Katie is tending to Sarah upstairs right now, the events of last night leaving the child traumatized and nearly catatonic. I've made plans for the two of them to leave for Spokane this afternoon, although Katie will surely fight me on it. On this I shall not be swayed.

Tillman has awakened an evil in Kobbe's End that I fear cannot be ignored nor contained, and I'll not lose another child to it.

The Tillman family did not grow, and that was a blessing, whether I knew it at the time or not. Richard, with little to do but mend the occasional broken bone or farm injury, spent more and more time at the lake which bore his name.

Not fishing, not bathing, but... studying. Surveying, dropping longer and longer sounding lines as he attempted to map the lakebed's topography. He seemed to be searching for something.

I realize now that naming me as the town's founder and Mayor was another indication of how diabolical Tillman could be. I was constantly solving municipal matters and bureaucratic issues, often requiring me to travel to Yakima or Seattle, and so I began to lose touch with the Tillman's, although Katie and Eva remained close, even when I could not be.

BUT I WAS here on that brutally hot September day when the spiders appeared.

I was shocked as any to wake to what seemed a layer of fine snow that morning, glittering as dawn broke.

The screams of the women - and some of the men, truth be told - was the first indication that things were not as they seemed, and I bade Katie to stay inside with the children while I investigated.

*Those who know me can attest that I am not a squeamish man, but the sheer volume of spiders that creeped and crawled across our roads, boardwalks, and buildings would have made any man pause that day. There seemed an unending variety of the creatures, thousands upon thousands of species of spider, each blacker, or hairier, or more bulbous than the last, and I must admit that I was well put off at the number of them.*

*As I attempted to quell the fears of the townsfolk, I noticed another peculiar fact - the spiders, en masse, had a destination. Whether on structure, hard pan, or field, they all crept in the same direction - the unfathomable lake that Tillman sleeps in now.*

*While Constable Johnson organized a clean up crew to sweep the buildings, I made my way through the woods, following the spiders, occasionally brushing my legs and jacket shoulders of the gathering arachnids, although it was apparent that they bore me no ill will, singularly focused as they were on their destination.*

*As I approached the open space surrounding the lake, an icy chill crept through my veins. The spiders were thicker here, crawling over each other and moving in thick, undulating carpets of tiny, black bodies. They crunched and crackled under my boots.*

*I exited the forest and stopped, bewildered. Even now I struggle to describe the astonishing phenomenon that was occurring in front of me.*

*The entirety of the lake shimmered in the rising sun, its surface completely covered by a blanket of fine spider silk. The water appeared to have frozen over, even as I felt the already daunting heat of the rising sun. In the center of that massive blanket of webbing was an opening, perhaps only a few feet in diameter, though it was difficult to tell from my distance.*

*And every spider that had landed in Kobbe's End, whether it the town proper, the surrounding woods, or the top of the lake, was scuttling and streaming into that hole, hurling and drowning their tiny bodies in the dark waters of Tillman's Depths.*

*Stranger still was the sight of Richard Tillman, nude at the water's edge, his bare skin smeared in glyphs of mud, or blood, or feces, I knew not what.*

*I approached him slowly, carefully, as you might a madman, for surely he must be mad to be standing such, filthy, unclothed, and heedless of the hundreds of spiders that crawled all over his bare skin.*

*"Richard," I said cautiously, reaching out to touch him.*

*He turned to me with a great, wide smile, and I was struck with the thought that I had never seen so joyous a look upon his face.*

*"Decraine," he said, genuinely happy to see me. He motioned to the silver-covered lake. "Can you hear it?"*

*I could hear nothing but the sound of tens of thousands of spider legs, crawling in unison, and told him so.*

"It's words," he explained. "I can almost understand them. She's waking up. She's trying to tell me something."

"Who's waking up?" I asked.

But Tillman merely turned back to the water without answering.

I GATHERED UP his clothing and shook the spiders from them, dressing him well enough to lead him home, where Eva received him, relieved, but not surprised when I told her how I'd found him. She promised to bathe him and make sure he was rested.

By the time I made it to my own door, the streets had been cleared of most of the spiders and their webbing, but my mind aches ferociously every time I think of those thousands upon thousands of tiny, bristly bodies, drowning themselves in that single, dark hole resting above Tillman's Depths.

The dreams began that night, hideous and horrifying visions, the details of which I could scant remember upon waking, although I knew that they centered around Richard Tillman and the waters which carry his name.

TILLMAN HIMSELF SEEMED rejuvenated by the happenings at the lake, insisting that the event was an omen of fabulous portent, and in the year following, it would have been hard to argue against it. The insects *and wasps that had troubled our crops and gardens were a thing of the past, thanks to our new spider population.*

*1885 was a banner year of growth, and Tillman proposed a festival on the anniversary of the spider migration, a celebration of the tiny creature that had reinvigorated our town.*

*It was met with some hesitancy, as one might expect, but eventually Tillman got his way. Eventually, Tillman always got his way.*

*That next year, as Richard began construction on the mansion that sits on the edge of the lake, Eva grew sick, a wasting illness that could be traced to no apparent cause.*

*I'd been spooked by what I'd seen on the day of the migration. Not just the bizarre phenomenon I'd witnessed at the lake, but also Tillman's strange behavior on the shore, as if he'd somehow set in motion the happenings himself. I'd begun shunning the lake and its namesake, but Katie and the girls would visit with Eva, returning home each time with sadder and sadder news of her health, and Katie finally convinced me to visit one last time with Richard and his wife before it was too late.*

TILLMAN HOUSE WAS *a monstrosity of a home when finished, and I thought it the height of vanity in size and scope, especially for a couple with no children. But when Richard opened the door at my knock, those feelings vanished in an instant, and I realized how much I had missed the man and our friendship.*

*We sat with whiskey for a spell, catching up on my municipal duties and Tillman's construction woes, but his gaze never left the view out the house's large, bay windows, from which nearly the entirety of the lake could be seen.*

*Richard finally turned to me again when I requested a short visit with Eva. He seemed ready to deny me, then acquiesced, leading me up the stairs to the room she had been confined to for the past several months.*

*I wasn't prepared for the sight of beautiful Eva reduced to a bedridden crone, her skin sallow and mottled and lifeless, her face aged much beyond her years, and spotted with strange and frightening welts.*

*My heart broke when she smiled and struggled to sit up in the bed, which Richard dutifully assisted her in accomplishing.*

*We shared only a few moments of small talk before the frail woman was overcome with a violent fit of coughing, and I excused myself, knowing that this was the last time I would see Eva Tillman alive.*

*If only that had been true.*


NEAR THE END of 1885, the population of Kobbe's End had grown to over 500 people. 500 men, women and children, working in fields and gardens, in the school, and the businesses that had begun to appear, including the recently built mill.

Our community had grown large enough that I could no longer remember the name and occupation of every resident, and had brought on a German fellow by the name of Zehnder as an assistant to help facilitate my municipal duties.

When Constable Johnson told me of Matthew Howard's disappearance, I couldn't at first place the man. But Johnson was clearly bothered by it, informing me that before Howard went missing, the farmer had complained of coyotes or wolves stealing a number of his goats, and the man was planning on standing watch and killing whatever animals he caught in the act.

"You think he was attacked by wolves?" I asked, unconvinced.

"The few wolves we've seen here have bolted immediately when confronted," Johnson told me, confirming my own thoughts. "There's no blood. Mister Howard is just... gone."

Johnson put together a small hunting party to scour the surrounding countryside, but nothing was found, wolf, goat, human, or otherwise.

Harold Hezel went missing shortly after, but he was a known drunk and the prevailing theory was that we'd find him someday, dead in the woods, having stumbled and cracked his skull open upon a stone or tree *stump. But they will not find him. I found him myself, last night, strung up in the attic of Tillman House.*

*Two days after Hezel had disappeared, the Forbeck boy and Andy Byers' little girl went missing from the homestead, and the town fell into a panic.*

*Was it one of our own? Had we let murderers into our community? During a town hall meeting, insults were hurled and a brawl broke out after the Callahan's claimed to have seen a devil crawling the roads two nights past. Constable Johnson and I were able to calm the meeting down, but the air hung heavy with charged nerves and frustrated parents.*

*MY OWN WORLD was shattered last night, beginning with Sarah's screams waking Katie and I from a troubled slumber of dark dreams. We rushed to the children's room to find Sarah huddled in the corner, eyes squeezed shut, unable to cease her terror-filled wailing.*

*Bewildered, I knelt next to my daughter, attempting comfort to no avail, until I saw my wife's face, eyes wide, mouth slack with horror. I followed her gaze, first to the empty bed where Christina should have been, and then to the open bedroom window, two floors above the ground outside.*

*I raced downstairs and out the door, fearful I'd see Christina's limp and broken form in the yard, and even more terrified to find that the ground was empty.*

*I called out for Christina repeatedly, the panic building and rising in my voice until I could contain it no more.*

*Racing back to the house, I climbed the staircase to the second floor, Sarah's wails still filling the air.*

*"Where is she?" I screamed, my volume overpowering Sarah's, but unable to cut through her terror.*

*I took the girl from Katie, who was openly weeping as well, and I shook my daughter forcefully.*

*"Sarah," I shouted, "Where is Christina? Where is your sister?"*

*Her eyes met mine, and I saw madness there, a void of insanity that chilled me to my bones.*

*I slapped the girl across the face then, in part with the hopes of breaking through that madness before it could take root, and in part because I was furious at the girl for drawing my own terror so close to the surface.*

*The slap halted Sarah mid-scream, and I saw recognition cross her features, finally. I held her face in both of my hands, staring directly into her eyes.*

*"Sarah," I implored, attempting to calm myself. "What happened to your sister?"*

*The young girl took two hitching breaths and whispered one word:*

*"Eva."*

I WOKE CONSTABLE *Johnson on my way to Tillman House. He grabbed his Winchester without a* word when he saw I was carrying my service rifle, and I filled him in on the night's events as we rode through the woods towards where I prayed we would find Christina, safe and unharmed.

I told Johnson of how I had found Tillman on the morning of the spider migration, leaving out my feelings that the man had somehow orchestrated the event himself, but impressing upon the constable that I felt Richard had gone mad, had perhaps been mad for many years.

We burst from the woods on the lake side of Tillman House and pulled up short. The house itself was silhouetted by the setting moon, an imposing sight, to be sure. More frightening still was the unearthly glow that emanated from the lake itself, as if a great, green torch had been lit at the bottom of those depths, pulsing in time to a strange, staccato beat that I felt deep within my bones.

Standing at the lake's shore was Richard Tillman, as I had found him the morning of the spider migration. He was nude, his body smeared and stained as before, arms raised above his head, fingers splayed.

The glow from the lake reflected in his eyes, deep, black pits filled to the brim with madness, and his voice rang out across the water, words and sounds that made no sense, that hurt my head and filled me with dread and seemed impossible to form with a human mouth.

"Iä Atlach-Nacha! Awaken, Mother Spider! Iä MictlŌntńcutli! Awaken, dream weaver!"

*With a shudder, I remembered Tillman's words to me on that cursed morning of the migration: "She's waking up."*

Johnson and I dismounted and I stormed towards Tillman, rifle in hand.

He didn't register me until I was nearly upon him. "Where is she?" I shouted, shoving him hard enough to knock him to the ground. "Where's Christina?"

He stared up at Johnson and I, confused at first, and then suddenly furious. "You fools! You'll ruin everything!"

"I'll ruin your goddamned head, you don't tell me where my daughter is! Where's Christina? Where's Eva?" I glanced up at the darkened house. "Are they up there?"

Something changed in Tillman's eyes then, a shift as he finally understood why I was there. It drove me to a berserker rage. I raised my rifle and pointed it at him, ready to pull the trigger if he didn't tell me where my sweet Christina was.

A heavy, white sack was suddenly tossed at my feet, and my mind neared to snap as I struggled to deny what I was seeing from the light of the lake's terrible, throbbing glow.

The sack was made of a frilly material, freshly and darkly stained, still wet, and spilling out of the sack's lace border was a tiny, lifeless arm. I stared at that arm in shock and horror, recognizing the delicate, tiny fingers as those of my dear Christina, and then realized the white, frilly sack was the nightdress she wore to bed, and that the stains...

"Here's your daughter," came a voice from the darkness. "Here's your precious Christina."

Somewhere in the back of my mind I recognized the voice as Eva's, but I could not tear my eyes from the torn and broken body of my little girl until Johnson began screaming next to me, his voice high and shrill enough to cut through my despair.

I followed his horrified gaze over my shoulder and felt my bladder let go at the sight that awaited me.

It was a spider, I suppose, or an entity so profoundly inhuman that "spider" is the nearest approximation I can muster.

But this spider towered over us, a great, bloated monster with a fat, bulbous abdomen held aloft by at least eight, hairy and multi-jointed legs.

This was the thing that lived in Tillman's Depths, I knew, that had killed little Christina and poor drunk Harold, and Matthew Howard and his goats, and the Byers and Forbeck children, I was sure of it. This was the thing that Tillman said was awakening... that Tillman was most likely responsible for awakening.

I stood trembling in my urine-soaked trousers, petrified, my rifle falling to my feet even as two of the monster's many limbs plucked me from the ground, lifting me up to examine me closer.

And in my terror, I realized I was wrong. This abomination did not come from the lake - at least, not entirely.

*Because the horror went deeper than that damned lake. From its dim, green glow, I recognized the features on the monster's all-too-human head. Smiling through a mouthful of sawblades was the face of Eva Tillman, beautiful again though surrounded by nightmare.*

"I didn't plan on Christina, tonight," Eva said, her voice raspy, demonic, as if human words were difficult to force through those multiple rows of teeth. "But I could feel her soft, lonely snoring as I crawled the roads, and I just couldn't resist!"

She smiled, and in the lake's glow I could see that her chin, her entire, devilish body was damp, shiny, covered in blood.

*My daughter's blood.*

I screamed then, and Eva laughed, delighted with my anguish. She had me in a grip of iron, and as much as I thrashed about, I could not break free.

"She was delicious," Eva continued, and lowered her face closer to me, her mouth opening wide, much too wide. "But I'm still so very HUNGRY!"

And then I heard the report of Johnson's Winchester, loud and very close, and Eva's beautiful face suddenly exploded and caved in, showering me with bits of bone and brain and blood.

The talons holding me spasmed, clutching me in an unbreakable death grip as Eva toppled, falling to the ground, dead.

Johnson rushed to me, face white as a sheet. He'd seen too much tonight. We both had.

He dropped to his knees next to me, prying Eva's sharp, deadly fingers from my arms. "That was Eva Tillman," I think he said, pulling me to my feet. The report of his Winchester still echoed in my head, a great ringing that even now has not completely left me. "But she's been taken by the dev-"

A frightful screaming interrupted him, and I gasped as Richard Tillman rose up from behind Johnson, gripping a heavy, glistening rock he'd pulled from the shore, and he brought that rock down with all his force on the top of Walter Johnson's skull.

I watched the light blink out of the constable's eyes in a flash and he fell, dead before he hit the ground. I was sure I would be Tillman's next victim, but the man dropped his bloody, makeshift weapon and fell to his knees next to the unholy corpse of his wife.

Tillman began to weep, rocking in anguish, whispering frenetically to Eva, and after a moment I realized he was not muttering words of sorrow, but a hushed, hurried version of what the man had been chanting only minutes earlier.

"Awaken Atlach-Nacha! Awaken, MictlŌntńcutli!"

I stared down at Constable Johnson, eyes wide open, brains spilling from his cracked skull; at the limp, broken shape of my innocent Christina; and the thought of Tillman pulling the strings of the last several years of my life, directing my actions and leading to all this death, filled me with a bloodthirsty rage. I wrapped the hand he had saved so many years ago around his devilish throat, squeezing with all my might.

He seemed not to notice at first, but as his windpipe began to collapse in my grip, he finally stood, choking and gasping and fighting me as I squeezed tighter and tighter.

His struggles led us to the water, where we fought and splashed until we were knee-deep in the lake, and I saw my chance.

I threw my weight and landed on top of him, forcing his head underwater, still gripping his throat.

The villain managed to break his head above the surface long enough to stare at me with eyes that bugged out of their sockets, and before I pushed his head back underwater, he choked out two words: "Rho Natus."

I held him there for several minutes, until I was sure he was dead, then dragged myself out of the water and collapsed on the shore, exhausted.

By the pulsing glow of the depths, I could see the silhouette of Tillman's corpse floating on the surface, pulled slowly by some phantom current towards the center of the lake.

I watched closely the man's body, still unsure of what happened next. One moment I could see Tillman's corpse, prone and unmoving, limbs splayed wide. And then... he was simply gone, dragged underwater by some unseen force.

Of what I found in the attic and library of Tillman House, I will not speak, nor shall I discuss the *horror of the basement well that tapped into the cursed waters of the lake, save only to say that what war and politics instilled in me - the belief that humankind had never been under the watchful care of a benevolent God- was last night reinforced a hundred times over.*

*There may very well be a God, but if so, it dwells at the bottom of Tillman's Depths, plotting humanity's demise.*

*ONCE KATIE AND Sarah are safely on their way, I shall return to Tillman House and destroy it. I am under no illusion that I will survive the night. My only wish is that I may end the Evil that dwells at the bottom of the lake.*

*Fulton's dynamite should do the trick.*

*I do this not only to avenge sweet Christina and the Forbeck boy and all the others, but to insure the safety of future generations of this town that is cursed with my name and my guilt.*

*It seems I'll be following Richard Tillman one last time, after all.*

*Decraine Kobbe.*
*August 9$^{th}$ 1885*

**The above document was found in a sealed envelope contained in Lot 16 of the Kobbe County Museum Auction: "Correspondence and various documents belonging to Decraine Kobbe." The auction was won by Mr. Peter Rawlik of Heather, WA.**

part four:

the gospel of
Rho Natus

# I

Peter Rawlik twice nearly lost control of his Tesla on the icy roads between Sunset and Kobbe's End, and twice had to remind himself that he'd gain nothing by dying before viewing the prize. He let pressure off the accelerator and tried to focus on his driving. But the falling snow was hypnotic in his headlights, and soon enough his thoughts were ricocheting between the desiccated corpse of the mutated boy he'd been shown in the tiny village on Lake Ananse in Ghana, and his regular visits to the 'End since he'd obtained the tantalizing writings of Decraine Kobbe.

His tires slid in the slush again as he stopped at the 'End's first blinking red light. The car handled fine for the rest of the short trip, including the sharp turn at the corner of the town's tiny park, where he'd observed evidence of Nancy Cook's miraculous recovery firsthand. He parked in the same stall he had occupied when Michael had brought him to visit Daniel several days ago. As impossible as it seemed, Rawlik suspected Nancy might somehow be going through a similar fantastic mutation as that young boy in Ghana.

After being shown that boy's corpse - a mishmash of multiple limbs and twisted, almost insect-like features, he'd been told by village elders the boy's horrific tale; his illness, his sudden recovery, his nightmarish transformation… and then his death at the hands of his own mother, who killed herself immediately after, leaving a suicide note consisting of only two words: *"Rho Natus."*

The strange case had sparked a fervor in him, a devotion that swiftly dwarfed his passion for the scripture, and then supplanted it, leading him to the strange story of Richard Tillman and his wife, Eva.

Rawlik stepped out of the Tesla, studying Serene Hope for a moment. He moved toward its front doors as he fished a small lock-picking kit from his jacket pocket.

In the dim light of the basement, Nancy cocked her gore-streaked head as Rawlik's picks scraped inside the front door's lock like an earthquake.

Hanging next to her was the freshly cocooned remains of Nikos DaBronzo, swinging lightly as she wound him slowly, tightly, round and round in her many arms, her spinnerets working constantly, producing a wet, silky substance that stiffened and thickened at exposure to oxygen.

She paused her work. It had been a busy night, full of surprises, and she'd cursed herself for not grabbing the other intruder from the backyard and dragging him down to the basement as well. Nikos would make for a fine, late-night snack in the future, but she had more immediate desires that required a living being.

And now it appeared she had been delivered precisely what she needed.

She left Nikos to twist slowly in the dim light, and then all her limbs were working in tandem to bring her silently up the basement stairs and into the kitchen.

The church was dark and silent, and Rawlik gripped the bar on the back side of the front doors, latching it closed behind him as quietly as possible. He pulled his cell phone out and toggled on the flashlight, making his way to the door that he had seen Daniel come rushing out of last week.

*What were you hiding, Daniel? I think I have an idea.*

The knob wouldn't turn, but the simple privacy lock was sprung easily with one of Rawlik's picks, and he let himself into the townhouse.

From the hallway, he felt an icy breeze and followed it to the kitchen, where his eyes were immediately drawn to the open door that looked out into the backyard beyond.

"Oh, no..." he moaned. Had she fled when Daniel left, taking advantage of his absence to make her escape? Or had Rawlik's own sudden, uninvited arrival scared her away just now? Had he blown his chance?

He walked towards the open door, slipping unexpectedly on the kitchen floor. Grasping the edge of the counter, he steadied himself and aimed the phone's flashlight at the slushy pink trail that snaked across the floor to the back door.

Rawlik side-stepped the slippery ribbon, peering into the backyard. The snow had been disturbed by many tracks, and a large smear, black in the darkness, that was slowly being obscured by the lightly falling flakes.

*Blood,* he thought, noting that the tracks and pink slush led *into* the church, not away from it.

He turned his light back to the kitchen floor, following its beam to the open basement door. As he crept closer, a dim glow from below attempted to illuminate the old wood stairs.

"Nancy," he called out. "Are you down there? It's all right. I'm an ally."

He began his descent into the basement, and Nancy, hidden in the shadows at the back of the hallway now, crept leg by leg onto the kitchen ceiling, soundlessly stalking him.

Rawlik could scarcely contain his excitement as he made his way down the narrow staircase, gently wiping a long spiderweb from out of his hair. He took a moment to rub the strand between his thumb and index finger, marveling at its substance and stickiness.

*Amazing.*

As he hit the bottom step, slipping again on the bloody slush, the beam from his flashlight fell upon the cardboard-and-gossamer nest in the far corner, and the relatively small spider hole at its base. He oriented his phone to portrait and turned on the camera.

"Oh baby," he whispered to himself, framing the nest in the viewscreen. "Look at you. You are magnificent."

The flashlight function shut off as the phone's camera flash took over, and a perfect still image of the nest popped up on its screen. He took a moment to admire it. *This changes everything.* "Good Lord. Absolutely incredible."

He reframed the shot once more, the flash popping over and over again as he got closer to the nest, and he didn't notice Nancy's eight crimson eyes reflected in the light until she was upon him.

# 2

Chitwood piloted his Bronco through the slushy streets of Kobbe's End and the morning snow that was still drifting down.

It had been a quiet night, and he appreciated the respite. He'd had just about enough of the drug deals, the domestic disputes, and the complaints about the homeless camp.

The uneventful night had given him the chance to reflect on Jeffrey Walsh, too. The Deputy, always a little weird, had been acting stranger than usual of late, distracted, angry.

Chitwood had suspected booze or pills at first. Lord knows he'd dabbled in both himself, and the current state of the world had everyone looking for an opportunity to check out for a while.

But it didn't feel right to Chitwood. Walsh wasn't a drunk, was never unaware of his surroundings. He just had something else on his mind. Something bigger than... well, Kobbe's End, apparently.

The sheriff still wasn't sure the kid was a good fit for the department. Walsh was certainly competent enough, but there was a darkness within him that kept Chitwood on edge.

He turned left on Bensen, kept his speed low as he approached Jenny's place. Taking the route past her house was almost automatic, and he dreaded the day he'd see an unfamiliar car parked next to hers in the driveway.

The breakup hadn't been the ugliest he'd been through - not even top five - but they'd each said a few words that would be impossible to walk back.

He could see that her Land Cruiser wasn't in the driveway, and he hated the sudden twist of jealousy, wondering where she might be so early in the morning. Had she spent the night somewhere else? With someone else?

Charlotte stood at the front gate, the Pom barking shrilly as he drove past, and he sped up, already embarrassed of the attention the dog's yips might bring. He didn't need anybody reporting back to Jenny that he'd been spotted cruising past her home.

*She hasn't been gone for long, at least. There's no way she'd leave Charlotte alone all night.*

But Chitwood had been an officer of the law for thirty-some years. He'd been trained well, back when that meant something, and he trusted his instincts, which were buzzing at him as he passed Jenny's house. They were telling him he had missed something.

He slowed the Bronco, finally stopping in the middle of the street in front of the house neighboring Jenny's. Checking to make sure the road behind was clear, he shifted the rig into reverse and backed up until he was directly in front of her driveway.

Charlotte continued to bark as he studied the house for a moment, then the yard, then the dog, trying to narrow down what was bothering him.

The dog being outside certainly wasn't the issue. Charlotte had run of the house and yard through a doggy door on the side entrance. His eyes shifted to the driveway, empty of Jenny's familiar green Land Cruiser, and covered in undisturbed snow.

She *had* been gone for a while. All night, at the very least. Her tire tracks should have been visible under the fresh snow, but there was no sign at all.

*She's an adult. She can do what she wants.* But she wouldn't leave Charlotte alone all night. He absolutely knew that for a fact. *She did this time. And she could be back at any minute.*

But it wasn't working for him. His gut was telling him something was off. He twisted the steering wheel sharply and pulled to the curb, parking directly in front of the house while Charlotte's barking intensified. If he was incorrect about this, he'd never live down the gossip of the sheriff's rig parked in front of his ex-girlfriend's house.

He snatched his phone from the passenger seat, scrolled to Jenny's name and pressed 'dial'.

The phone rang on the other end and then went to voicemail. Chitwood hung up without leaving a message.

He looked over at Charlotte, hopping and barking at the gate near the sidewalk, then probed the gap in his teeth with his tongue as he contemplated his next move.

Daniel's head was pounding from last night's drinks, and his anxiety continued to grow as Michael's Suburban brought them closer and closer to Kobbe's End.

He remembered arriving at Michael's posh rambler in Heather last night, remembered the surprised look on his friend's face, remembered the warm response to Daniel explaining that he could really use a friend right now, a sympathetic ear.

And then the Scotch came out, and Daniel, a notorious lightweight, found the remainder of the evening's discussion rather fuzzy.

*That's called a blackout, you idiot.*

He wasn't sure precisely what he'd told Michael, but it couldn't have been the truth about Nancy's strange metamorphosis. If it had, then his friend had clearly (and thankfully) not believed him. Whatever he'd revealed, though, had Michael insisting he return to Kobbe's End with Daniel.

As they drove, the molten pit in Daniel's stomach continued to churn.

He'd agreed that bringing the K-Car back was a dangerous prospect. Still, he obviously could not allow Michael entrance to the church to see Nancy. She was far too dangerous now, too unpredictable. And what would Michael do when faced with the truth of what Nancy had become? With what Daniel had done to accommodate her?

Daniel would simply have to tell Michael, in no uncertain terms, that the man was not welcome inside.

*Thanks for the ride, my friend. Now kindly fuck off.*

That would certainly raise suspicions, but it was clearly past time for Daniel and Nancy to leave Kobbe's End, anyway. It had to happen tonight.

His thoughts kept drifting to the long line of freight trains that rumbled regularly through the 'End. With the mill and the mines long abandoned, the trains had no reason to stop in town anymore. Still, Daniel thought there must be some way to sneak Nancy into one of those cars, hobo-style. Her new form would definitely require something bigger than the K-Car, which he had abandoned in Michael's driveway in Heather, regardless.

Michael continued to drive in silence, and had been acting strangely all morning, checking his phone obsessively, always unsatisfied with the results, fueling Daniel's anxiety.

"Everything okay?" Daniel asked.

"Just fine," Michael assured him, eyes never leaving the road.

*Definitely not fine,* Daniel thought.

He turned his gaze away from the grimy, snow-covered houses in the 'End's morning light as they rounded the sharp corner that brought Serene Hope into view. But as they pulled in, he was seized in an unbreakable grip of absolute despair. A black Tesla with a fine dusting of snow was parked in front of the church.

"No, no, no," Daniel said, realizing now why Michael had been checking his phone all morning. "What is this?"

"It's Doctor Rawlik," Michael said calmly. "I asked him to check on Nancy. It'll be fine, I promise."

As he pulled on his door handle, Daniel reached across and stopped him. "Michael," he said, "You have no idea what you've done. You've betrayed one friend… and killed another."

Michael shook his head, disappointed. "Stop it. Just stop it. I'm not letting you go through with this, Daniel. You're not going to kill Nancy."

"I'm not going to…" Daniel felt the pieces he was missing finally fall into place, and he rushed after his friend, who was out of the Suburban and already through the gate of the church's backyard.

*He thinks I'm going to perform some kind of "mercy killing" on Nancy,* Daniel realized. *And he's determined to stop me from forfeiting my eternal soul.*

*How very Michael.*

Both men slowed at the sight of the open kitchen door, but Daniel's heart bottomed out, his suspicions confirmed as he realized what the barely concealed, pink trail under the fresh layer of snow must mean: Rawlik had shown up at the behest of Michael and Nancy had dispatched of him without a second thought.

*Wait… are those Nancy's pill bottles?*

He shook the thought away and followed Michael into the kitchen, slowly now, both of them eyeing the broken, open basement door.

"No," Daniel whispered. "Dammit, no."

Michael turned to face him. "What exactly is going on here?" he asked. "Are you telling me that Nancy is in the basement…"

"Michael," Daniel replied, "You must leave. *Now.*"

"Good Lord. What were you thinking." Michael strode directly to the yawning basement door. "Peter! Nancy! Are you down there?"

"Don't," Daniel said. "She'll hurt you."

Michael sneered back at him, disgusted, then made his way down the basement stairs and towards the dim light below.

Chitwood opened the Bronco's door, pocketing the truck's keys. He'd waited long enough, and his unease had only continued to grow.

Charlotte hopped excitedly on the other side of the gate as he approached, making the sheriff still more uncomfortable. Normally the dog would be furious about someone nearing the fence, but the Pom was eager, ecstatic to see him. Relieved, even.

"Hey girl," he said, reaching a hand over the gate to her. The dog whined and licked gratefully at his palm.

He opened the gate and closed it behind him as he stepped into the yard and made his way to the snow-covered garden bed near the front door, Charlotte following enthusiastically behind.

The dog pressed up against his leg as he kneeled and cleared snow from the bed, and he could feel her trembling as he continued to search, search… *there it is.*

Picking up the rock he'd found, he brushed snow and dirt away from it and thumbed open the slot that held the spare key. He'd often teased Jenny about how obvious the fake rock had looked, but was glad now to find it still there.

Charlotte raced through the doggy door and was waiting for Chitwood in the living room when he let himself in.

The house felt cold, empty. He did a quick walk-through, relieved to find no sign of a break-in or anything nefarious.

He followed the sound of Charlotte's yips into the kitchen, where the dog was making frantic circles around her empty food and water bowls.

The water dish he filled first, and she lapped thirstily at it when he set it down. From the pantry, he scooped a cup of dry dog food and tipped it into Charlotte's food bowl. The Pom devoured it immediately.

Wade watched her eat for a moment, collecting his thoughts. Jenny had no close family he could reach out to, but he knew she was friendly with many of the officials and business owners in the 'End. He could start there.

Turning to leave, Chitwood's gaze caught the slip of paper on the kitchen's counter.

His eyes narrowed as he recognized her familiar, thin scrawl, and he leaned over to read:

> *To Whom it May Concern:*
> *I have a very bad feeling about Nancy Cook and her husband, Daniel.*
> *If I'm missing, please check Serene Hope first.*

*Oh, Christ,* Chitwood thought. *You and your fucking true-crime bullshit.* They'd argued about her fascination with murder and he'd even accused her of being a badge bunny during their breakup fight.

*Yeah,* he thought, *but she* is *missing. And she left a very clear note of where to find her. Smart girl.*

He locked her front door and pocketed the spare key. Charlotte came busting out of the doggy door, unwilling to be abandoned again, but Chitwood blocked the gate with his leg, denying her exit and shutting her back in. The little Pom barked frantically as he got back into the Bronco and keyed the mic on his radio.

"Dispatch," he said, "Standby. Thought I heard a commotion at Serene Hope Church. Repeat, standby."

There was a pause that angered Chitwood immediately. He was about to key the mic button again when his radio squawked obnoxiously.

"Rodger," came Deputy Walsh's voice. "Standing by."

Both pastors reached the basement floor, Michael squinting to see the jumble of melting boxes in one corner and the massive pile of trash in the other. He couldn't hide his disgust. "God, man," he said, hand to his mouth. "Is she down *here*? In all this filth?"

"It's not like that," Daniel protested.

Michael ignored him. He snatched an old yardstick from where it leaned against the concrete wall and began swinging and batting at the webs and cocoons, trying to clear a path.

"Don't do that," came Nancy's voice from the darkness, firm and commanding.

Michael stopped immediately, his eyes darting back and forth, searching for the source of the voice. "Nancy," he said, "Where are you?" He started swinging the yardstick urgently, aiming in the direction he thought the voice had come from. "Nancy? It's okay, I'm going to get you out of here. Where's Peter?"

"I SAID DON'T DO THAT!"

She dropped from the ceiling directly in front of him, beautiful and horrifying, her face a mask of rage and fury. Michael rocked back on his heels and stumbled, falling on his ass as Nancy's monstrous new form hung suspended over him.

"Nancy!" Daniel yelled. "No! Don't hurt him!"

Nancy's great, spidery legs trembled above the fallen holy man, and she spun deliberately to face Daniel with a sly smile. "Why is he here," she said, "if not to feed me?"

Daniel glanced at his old friend, lying nearly prone on the dusty concrete floor, both hands extended to ward the devil-monster away.

"He's not supposed to be here," Daniel said. "I just... I needed to talk to somebody. Counsel. Guidance."

Michael staggered to his feet. He was terrified, ready to bolt. "Fuck your guidance!"

Nancy twisted easily towards him, her mouth opening, ratcheting wide, wide, impossibly wide.

"Such language, Michael," came the unexpected voice of Peter Rawlik. Both men whirled to face the doctor as he crawled from the tiny spider-hole in Nancy's nest.

Daniel gasped audibly at the sight of the man. He was completely nude, his skin covered in multiple scars and tattoos. Frightening in itself, but the state of the doctor's body horrified Daniel even more. The man was still a giant, perhaps only four or five inches shy of seven feet, but his muscular frame seemed wilted, wasted, his once handsome face a maze of sagging wrinkles.

Daniel watched as the big man's color seemed to fade and turn ashen. Rawlik was dying in front of their eyes, his skin flattening and drying with almost supernatural speed, as if there were a giant straw slammed into his back, and something huge and infinitely evil was sucking powerfully at the opposite end.

His eyes were dark pits in that fleshy puzzle, shining with hate and madness. Daniel wondered what the man had seen in Nancy's nest, that horror show of cardboard and gossamer angles that baffled the senses from the outside. He feared it might somehow be bigger on the inside. Perhaps boundless.

The doctor's abdomen was wrapped with what appeared to be frayed bandages, as if Rawlik's ribs had been broken and bound years earlier, but as the naked man strode towards them, Daniel could see that what he thought were bandages were streamers of the thick silk that Nancy had somehow created her massive basement web with.

*What have you been up to, Nancy?*

"Peter," Michael said uncertainly. "What are you doing?"

The doctor stepped closer, frightening, threatening. In one hand he held a wickedly sharp chef's knife that Daniel absently recognized from the cheap wooden knife block that sat next to the microwave upstairs.

Rawlik glared at the two of them. "I'm certainly not letting you sound some kind of hysterical alarm on the most important find of all time."

Daniel attempted to solve the puzzle, but there were just too many pieces, and nothing made any sense. "Nancy," he murmured, "What's going on?"

She smiled at her husband, all needles and razor blades. "Doctor Rawlik introduced himself to me last night. I was going to eat him, but he seemed quite sincere. And more than willing to serve, once I explained… *the situation.*"

Rawlik stepped closer and in the feeble light, Daniel could make out some of his tattoos. They looked tribal, powerful. Evil. The scarring that surrounded them was deliberate, symbols and shapes that had been purposefully carved into the big man's skin some time ago.

The most prominent of the tattoos spanned the width of Rawlik's chest, deep black ink in tribal lettering that read simply, *Rho Natus*. It sent an electric jolt through Daniel's entire being.

"She understands that I'm not here to hurt her," Rawlik said. "That I wouldn't let *anyone* hurt her."

"Hurt her?" Michael shouted, defiant. "For Christ's sake, man… she's a monster!"

Rawlik spun on the old pastor, the kitchen knife pointing accusingly. Daniel could see that the doctor's back was covered in an elaborate spider tattoo that wrapped both shoulders and trailed down to his buttocks.

"You're the monster," Rawlik screamed at Michael, his voice cracking, raspy. "You and your outdated beliefs! Look at her, you old fool! Do you think something like this happens accidentally? This is Intelligent Design! This is Theistic Evolution! This is the power of God at work!"

Nancy grinned again at the compliment, displaying her terrifying and deadly teeth. Her many limbs twitched and pulsated eagerly, as if she could barely keep herself from stroking the doctor.

"She is not something to be feared," Rawlik shouted. "She is not something to be hated! She is something to be worshipped!"

Daniel couldn't believe what he was hearing, what he was seeing. *Is my spider-monster wife and a dying, naked giant with a chef's knife really teaming up in the basement of my church? How has life twisted so thoroughly into this madness?*

Rawlik gestured with the butcher knife at his scars and tattoos. "I have identified myself as an apostle! Can you not see the Messiah when she's right in front of your eyes?"

Michael's mouth dropped open. "Good Lord... you're insane. You think this... this creature is the Second Coming? If anything, she is *unholy*! A demon from Hell!"

Daniel watched his wife try to feign hurt, but she couldn't quite hide how amused she was at the turn the situation had taken.

"You're a blind idiot," Rawlik said. "*You're* insane. A slave to the writings of superstitious primitives. 'The Second Coming'? Of course not. She is the *only* Messiah, the avatar of Atlach-Nacha!"

Daniel glanced over at Nancy and she seemed to roll all eight of her dull, red eyes at him. Even she thought Rawlik was a wack-job, but the proceedings obviously entertained her.

"Enough of this," Michael said. "You're all mad!" He made a break for the stairs, attempting to push past the doctor. But Rawlik lunged, grabbing Michael by the shoulder and burying the butcher knife to the hilt in the man's stomach. He yanked it out with savage glee, and Michael's shirt blossomed crimson. The old man shrieked in agony, doubling over and clutching at his stomach.

A whimpered, "no..." escaped Daniel's lips, and he stumbled back, shocked, useless, unable to do anything but watch the horrible scenario play out.

As Michael staggered away from Rawlik, the withering giant reached out, grabbing the old man by his hair and pulling him upright just long enough to slide the butcher knife across the pastor's throat. Michael lashed out, breaking the doctor's grip, hands grasping at his neck, which gurgled and whistled through great gouts of blood. He spun around wildly and fell to the floor, fingers fluttering weakly around his throat for a few seconds, before falling still.

Daniel stared at his dead friend, his mind see-sawing, his chest hitching as he tried to breathe, to scream, to do anything. He was petrified with horror and despair, rooted to the basement floor.

Nancy scrutinized him with her otherworldly gaze, studying Daniel's reaction. His trauma, his madness. His *humanity*. It all seemed so foreign to her now.

Rawlik, chest and arms smeared with Michael's gore, the bloody butcher knife trembling weakly in his hands, took three long strides across the basement towards Daniel.

"And you," he said, his voice dripping with scorn and hate. "You miserable coward. Charged with protecting the fate of the world, responsible for the single most important being on the planet in the history of all mankind..."

He stumbled towards Daniel and the pastor retreated, bumping his head on hanging cocoons until his back pressed against the basement wall and the interconnected web system around them was vibrating chaotically.

Daniel's eyes darted left and right, searching for anything he might defend himself with. There was nothing.

Rawlik reared above Daniel, his eyes completely mad. "You don't deserve the honor," he rasped through failing vocal cords, spittle flying. "Worse, you can't handle the responsibility. You are a weak link, a Judas in the inner circle, and I will not allow that."

Daniel flinched, looking away as the dying man raised the kitchen knife above his head. But the blow never landed.

Instead, the knife fell, clattering against the floor. Rawlik stumbled, gasping for air. He dropped to his knees in front of Daniel, his chest heaving, stomach bulging against the webbing that had been tightly wrapped around his midsection.

Nancy crawled across the ceiling, her body pulsing with excitement, her eyes locked on the dying man, thrilled, entranced, absolutely delighted with what she was seeing, and Rawlik took his last wheezing breath.

She turned her suddenly shiny eyes towards Daniel, noting the horror on his face, and she crawled down the wall to crouch next to her husband.

"My love," she said, "Don't let his words bother you. He meant nothing to me. A distraction. A fling. You're still the man I love…"

She reached one hairy, multi-knuckled hand down to Rawlik's dead body, tenderly stroking his wrapped, distended torso.

"…and the father of our children."

It hit Daniel then, the implication. The chasm in his mind grew wider, the blackness swallowing him completely. He stumbled and nearly fell, then righted himself and made his way unsteadily up the basement stairs.

Nancy watched him as he climbed, and a dry, spidery chuckle slipped past her lips. Then she turned back to Rawlik's dried and desiccated corpse. His wrinkled face was turned toward her, eyes wide open, so that he might adore her forevermore.

Daniel staggered out of the basement and directly to the kitchen sink, vomiting stinging bile and last night's whiskey out of his system. "Oh, God," he repeated between bouts of violent heaving. "Michael… please, no… I'm so sorry…"

He turned the tap on, splashing cold water onto his face and into his mouth, then stumbled out of the kitchen, stepping over the trail of Nikos's blood and teetering into the church proper. Lurching down the threadbare carpet, he used the backs of each pew to steady himself and finally fell to his knees in front of the giant abstract cross behind his lectern.

He stared up at it, tears streaming down his cheeks. "Oh, Father, please. Please. I am lost and I do not know what to do."

He wailed in anguish. The shocking murder of his oldest friend had been too much. The sheer amount of horror and death and insanity occurring in his church over the past few weeks was impossible for him to fathom, and the revelation that he and Nancy would finally have children was a cruelty he couldn't even begin to process. What had he done to bring this misery upon himself and the people of his town? "Forgive me for forsaking you. Only tell me the reason this is happening. Tell me what I must do. I cling tightly to you. I… I…" His prayer dissolved into sobs.

There was no answer, and Daniel understood God had judged him unworthy. As a man *and* a husband.

He took a few hitching gulps of air, his breathing finally slowing. Over the next few minutes, the tears dried on his face and he climbed from the pit of roiling black snakes that nested in his brain, watching the sunlight crawl languidly across the threadbare carpet. He was left with a cold certainty of what needed to be done. The clarity he'd been pleading for was presented to him in no uncertain terms, and as was almost always the case, it was simple and obvious. He'd taken a vow before God to love and protect his wife, in sickness and in health.

Nothing had changed.

"Daniel?" Above him, Nancy's gore-streaked face crept from behind the cross She studied Daniel stonily, completely detached from humanity.

*Spidermind.*

Daniel's composure threatened to crumble again, his chin falling to his chest. He balled his fists and pressed them against his eyes until he saw stars. "So much death, Nance. So much death."

She cocked her head, studying him. "And life," she said. "Our children are nearly here. And they will live. Live to carry on our legacy."

The canyon in Daniel's mind yawned violently again. He hadn't allowed himself to consider the future. "Yes," he mumbled. "Yes. Our children." He gazed up at Nancy's beautiful face, the face he had fallen in love with so many years earlier. If he ignored her many eyes, her terrifying teeth, he could almost see the woman he married.

*The woman whom Michael had married him to.* Daniel dropped his gaze. "Our friends," he groaned. "You can't keep killing our friends. You just... *can't keep killing.*"

"They weren't our friends," Nancy said, her eyes flashing angrily. "Michael called me a monster! Besides, Rawlik killed him, not I."

Daniel almost laughed. "Rawlik," he said. "Michael. Jenny. Whoever else. It has to stop, Nancy. I can't keep doing this..."

"Of course," she said, her harmonized voice eerie but soothing, almost hypnotic. "Of course. Whatever you need, my love."

Daniel turned up to face her. "To leave," he said. "We need to leave."

"Leave the church?"

"Leave the 'End. We can't stay here. You can't just eat your way through the entire town."

Nancy canted her head again. She looked as if the idea of eating the entire town was not the worst she'd ever heard. "Where would we go?" she asked. "How would we even do it?"

"Olympic National Forest," Daniel answered. "It's big enough. Ridiculously huge. Big enough for you to live free. And enough game for... hunting."

"Big enough for our children," Nancy said, the idea taking root as she pictured the many hikers on the trails where they'd vacationed so many years ago.

"Yes," Daniel said. "For all of us. We can take Michael's Suburban. It'll be tight, but you'll fit in the back if we remove the seats. I'll block out the windows. We can make the drive in a day."

"Rawlik has to come as well," she reminded him.

"Of course," Daniel said, imagining the smell of the dead man inside the vehicle after a twelve-hour drive.

"Nothing must happen to him."

"It will be fine. I'll get the truck ready."

Nancy grinned, and Daniel almost convinced himself that he couldn't see the gore between her saw-blade smile.

"I love you," she said, and he almost believed her.

"I love you back," he said, surer of it than ever. He headed for the doors at the end of the church.

He pressed down on the bar, unlatching the door, then nearly fell back, startled to find Sheriff Chitwood in the doorway, hand on one of the big, outside handles. Behind him at the snowy curb was his old Bronco, parked next to Rawlik's Tesla and Michael's Suburban.

Daniel let out a surprised "oh!" and tried to block as much of the view into the church as he could.

"Oh, hey," Chitwood said through his thick mustache and missing tooth. "Sorry to just drop in on you like this, Father."

"Pastor," Daniel corrected automatically, heart racing again. Surely no heart was meant to withstand the kind of strain his own had been under these past two weeks. "What can I do for you, sheriff?"

Chitwood ran a palm down his mustache and stepped closer. "Well," he drawled, "I hope it's not a bad time, but I need to ask you some questions."

Daniel held his ground. *This is how it ends, Nancy,* he thought. *We've been lucky, but it's finally run out.*

"Okay," Daniel said, trying to gauge a correct amount of surprise and innocence. "What's going on?"

"Well, I'm trying to get a hold of Jenny Thomas."

Daniel kept his face neutral but could feel the muscle beneath his right eye begin to twitch. He watched the sheriff's very relaxed, friendly face, the face of a man you could trust.

*Except for his eyes,* Daniel thought. *No, his eyes don't seem very friendly at all right now.*

"Jenny?" he said. "Well, she's not here." *Not anymore.* "Have you tried her house?"

"I sure did," Chitwood said. "She seems to have gone missing. And I'm a little concerned. Thought I'd check with some of her friends, see if they'd seen her lately. I know you were close with her."

"Well," Daniel said, trying to blot out the memory of Jenny's bootless foot being dragged into Nancy's nest. "She was at the Sunday service, of course. But I haven't seen her since then. She *is* an adult. Probably just visiting friends. Maybe in Heather or Sunset?"

"Sure, sure," Chitwood said, sucking air through the gap in his teeth. "I thought of that. But the reason I'm worried is that her dog, Charlotte - you know Charlotte? - anyway, she left Charlotte alone. And she just wouldn't do that."

*Christ,* Daniel thought, *I'm going to regret not letting Nancy have the dog.* "Yeah," he said. "Good point. She definitely wouldn't leave Charlotte alone." He rubbed a hand across his chin, realizing he hadn't shaved in a week or more.

"I don't know what to tell you. But please keep me in the loop. I hope nothing's happened to her."

The bigger man crowded in on Daniel, and he finally backed up, feeling a surge of panic as Chitwood made his way into the church, smiling politely the entire time.

Daniel risked a glance towards the ceiling and Chitwood's eyes followed, but Nancy was thankfully nowhere to be seen.

"You know," the sheriff said, "I'd really like to talk to Mrs. Cook. Maybe Jenny said something to her more recently? I know she's been very ill, but maybe Jenny called her, mentioned going out of town or something?"

Daniel's mind raced. "Nancy? No. She's not here. Visiting friends in Heather."

Chitwood studied him for a moment, then pulled a little notebook and pen from the inside pocket of his heavy jacket, jotted something down in it. He glanced back up at Daniel nonchalantly, just making conversation. "I thought she was very sick. Bedridden."

Daniel's mouth went dry. "She's doing much better," he said carefully. "A miracle, I suppose. And visiting friends, now."

"I'm sure you can get me their contact info before I leave."

"What's going on here? Am I in trouble?"

"Oh God, no, padre," Chitwood said. "I'm just dotting my tees and crossing my eyes. I mean, if something happened to Jenny, I want the record to show that I did everything by the book." He gave Daniel a conspiratorial glance. "We had a pretty ugly breakup, you know. I don't want anyone saying I didn't do my best work."

"Of course," Daniel said, the muscle under his eye jitterbugging wildly.

Chitwood cast one more glance around the church and turned to leave. "Ah, one more thing, padre?"

Daniel wanted to scream. He said, very calmly, "Yes?"

"Can I use your restroom?"

Wade watched the little man's eyes turn to flint. *He's going to push,* he thought. *Disarm him now.*

"I've been fighting a UI," the sheriff explained, putting on his best "embarrassed old man" act. "Maybe kidney stones. Hell, I don't know. Maybe just my prostate. I should probably swing by the clinic and have Carpenter check me out. Regardless, it means I have to piss every seven and a half minutes."

Chitwood knew he should leave and head directly to Judge Wicklund for a search warrant. He had Jenny's note and a very suspicious-acting Daniel Cook, and his own gut was screaming at him. Jenny was right. The minister had killed his wife, and Jenny had confronted him. Her reward was most likely murder.

But what if she were still alive? Any delay now could mean her life. Cook was soft, weak. Chitwood had no fear of the smaller man attacking him and if he could get into the townhouse he might find probable cause to end this right now.

The pastor smiled thinly. "Sure," he said, shoulders visibly slumping. He walked Chitwood to the door that led to the living space.

Wade scoped Daniel's body language like a hawk when the man opened the door to a slender hallway, guiding him to the right and not-so-subtly blocking his way to the left.

"Right down there," the minister said, his voice tight.

The sheriff nodded and smiled, looking past Daniel to the light coming from the kitchen at the end of the hall.

"What's down there?" Chitwood said, his voice hard.

"Nothing," Daniel said. "The kitchen."

Chitwood abruptly stopped, grabbing Daniel tightly, the end of his fingers nearly touching as they wrapped around the small man's bicep. "Everything okay, padre?" he asked. "Anything you want to tell me right now?"

He could feel the pastor's body tense, fight-or-flight kicking in, and he tightened his grip painfully on Daniel's arm. "Don't do it," he warned, marching Daniel in front of him into the kitchen.

"You don't need to do this," Daniel said, his panic rising. He took in the kitchen with fresh eyes as Chitwood forced him into a chair at the dining table. He imagined what it must look like to the sheriff: vomit in the sink, a bloody trail from the kitchen door to the damaged basement door… which was now closed.

"Who else is here?" Chitwood barked at him.

"Nobody," Daniel said, feeling the world spinning completely out of control. "Nobody! Just leave! Leave while you can!"

"Don't you lie to me," Chitwood hissed, his eyes hard as stone, and Daniel realized that this had become very personal. Ugly breakup or not, the sheriff still loved Jenny very much.

*He has his hand on his gun and I think he's going to pull it,* Daniel thought, *pull his weapon and shoot me right where I sit. And that would be just fine, that would solve all my problems right now, wouldn't it?*

And then there came the *thump.*

Chitwood spun immediately to the basement door, taking in the splintered jamb, the hastily installed and hanging loop lock. He turned back to Daniel. "What's behind that door?"

*A monster,* Daniel almost said, but what came out instead was a whispered, "The basement."

The sheriff took his hand off the butt of his holstered weapon and keyed the button on the mic attached to his shoulder. "This is Chitwood," he said. "Requesting backup at Serene Hope."

Deputy Jeffrey Walsh sat behind the old, gnarled station desk, staring at the chunky police radio that shared desk space with the outdated department computer which had automatically logged Chitwood's request for backup.

Walsh hadn't slept a wink last night, having finally driven home after kneeling in the church's backyard for who knows how long. He'd hoped that magnificent creature would return and bestow its wisdom upon him, somehow directing him towards his purpose in the new era Kobbe's End was racing towards.

But there was no further contact. If not for the massive pool of gore at the bottom of the steps, there would be no sign of the miracle he'd witnessed.

*An angel,* he thought. *Or a devil. It didn't matter. The existence of one proved the other.*

The question now was what was the most effective means of service? Was he disciple or apostle? Student of this new religion, or messenger?

Despondent, he'd finally gone home, shedding his sopping wet pants and shoes, then masturbated furiously, imagining over and over again the anguished scream that had been torn from Nikos as he'd been brutally ripped in half, and when Walsh finally climaxed, he'd mimicked that haunting sound as best he could.

His release hadn't lessened the certainty that events were coming to a head in Kobbe's End, and Walsh - certain he'd witnessed the avatar of the God in the Lake - had no idea if fulfilling his purpose required his sacrifice or his survival in order to ensure the success of the coming apocalypse.

The feeling persisted, growing until it was time for his work shift to begin, and he was gripped with the certainty he was needed at the station and that his presence was imperative. Not to fulfill his office duties for the first three hours of his scheduled shift, but for a bigger scheme, a grander, more important plan that he knew to be pure, but did not yet understand.

He'd arrived at the station and that asshole Anthony immediately started up with his bullshit.

They'd both joined the Department around the same time but had never really connected. Anthony projected an air of confidence, and he had an opinion about everything, whether music, film, or politics, his taste directly opposed to Walsh's at every turn.

Anthony had been alone at the station for his first hour and was clearly eager to have an audience. When Walsh showed up, the other deputy began pontificating on the purpose of dreams and how to decipher them, citing the nightmares he'd been having for the last few weeks. From there he segued into headache remedies, explaining he'd been suffering from them since he'd first moved to the 'End, and wondering if the station's furnace might be responsible for creating a troublesome amount of carbon monoxide.

Walsh said nothing and Anthony finally grew tired of the one-sided discussion. He went back to converting years of Kobbe County paperwork to digital, as the station attempted to finally catch up to the 21st century.

Walsh fussed and fidgeted for the next hour, hyper-aware of every air current and eddy, every sound as the building settled around him and the electricity in the air mounted.

And then Chitwood's call came. He was "poking around" the church for some reason.

*The church! It's happening!*

Anthony popped his head over the top of the computer, his eyes meeting Walsh's. "A little late for the boss to find religion, isn't it?"

Walsh responded with a thin smile and a mumbled, "Probably just some kids." Inside, his thoughts were frenzied. He wanted to jump in his vehicle, head over right then, be there when Chitwood discovered... *whatever* it was he was going to discover.

He couldn't help but imagine what would happen to the sheriff when he crossed the threshold of that holy place. Chitwood was a hardass, yes. But he was also a Boy Scout. He stood no chance against the being that occupied the church.

And if Walsh showed up and somehow misidentified himself as an ally to the sheriff in the eyes of the creature that had shown him grace and mercy last night? That seemed like an easy way to turn from apostle to heretic pretty damn quick.

But then Chitwood's second call came in, this time requesting backup.

"Holy shit," Anthony said, and Walsh watched him reach for the "speak" button on his desk mic. "Copy," he said into the mic. "Unit 8 responding, in transit immediately. Two minutes."

He stood quickly, checking his belt and holster, then looked to Walsh, eyes bright and eager.

Walsh had his service .45 aimed squarely at Anthony's face. He took a moment to savor the other deputy's confusion, then squeezed the trigger.

The gun roared and bucked in his hand and Anthony flew backwards, feet leaving the ground. Behind him, the wall of Safety Instructions, Employee Rights, and Law Enforcement awards was splattered with blood and brains and hairy bits of his skull.

Walsh lowered his pistol, savoring the smell of cordite, rolling his neck to release the tightness there.

He walked over to Anthony, noting the small hole under the man's right eye, congratulating himself on his marksmanship.

Anthony's left eye stared directly at Walsh, and with a start he realized the man was still alive, his mouth trying to move, to form words.

"Oh, wow," Walsh said, and he squatted next to the deputy for a closer examination.

A pool of thick, dark blood was spreading from the back of Anthony's head, and Walsh felt a flush of excitement as the shine left the dying man's one, good eye.

"Awesome," he said after a moment, still not believing it.

*My first kill,* he thought, with no small amount of pride.

*First of many, you fuckin rockstar.*

He stood and turned towards the computer log screen. It was splattered with blood, and he watched the green cursor blink at the end of the code that had automatically been logged with Chitwood's LE ID and his two reports over the last thirty minutes.

Quickly, Walsh highlighted both reports with the mouse and hit the 'DEL' key, smiling as they disappeared. It wasn't a permanent change - that was impossible - but it would take a while for anyone to notice, what with the carnage splattered all over the office.

Walsh suddenly realized he'd played his part. This was what the lake had required of him. No further action was necessary. He could stay to see how it all shook out if he liked, but he had a feeling it might be a good goddamned time to leave Kobbe's End to whatever fate The Universe had in store for the tiny town. He could still spread the Gospel of Rho Natus from Idaho or Oregon or even California or Nevada, for that matter.

Jeffrey Walsh thought he might be ready for a change of weather.

"Think hard before you decide to do something stupid, padre," Chitwood said. He had Daniel's bony shoulder gripped tightly in one meaty hand, guiding the pastor in front of him down the wooden steps to the basement. The other hand held his sheriff-issued Mag Lite - eighteen inches of heavy, black aluminum and six D-Cell batteries - its halogen beam illuminating swaying webs and floating dust motes. "You don't want to get clocked with this. Cave your fucking skull right in."

He lightly tapped the flashlight against Daniel's head to illustrate his point. The man flinched but said nothing. Chitwood knew he should wait for his backup to arrive and was relieved it was Anthony that had responded instead of Walsh, but he still felt time was of the essence.

"Hello," Chitwood called out. "Officer of the Law. Answer if you are able." And then, against his better judgment, "Jenny? You down here, honey?"

They reached the concrete floor and his eyes widened at the sheer amount of debris and detritus scattered around the basement, the stains and piles of clothing his Mag Lite illuminated at every turn. The filth suggested that nothing had been down here in years. So why was the minister so nervous? Why were his own nerves jangling at full volume?

The light flashed across a massive pile of boxes in one corner, and Chitwood swung the beam slowly back to rest on everything that was wrong with it; the angles that hurt his eyes to even consider, the tiny hole at the bottom of the pile.

"Jesus Christ," he said, disgusted. "What the fuck…" He had a terrible feeling about what he'd find if he looked in that hole, but he skirted around the damp and dirty pile to try to get a glimpse, steering Daniel in front of him the entire time.

The side of his head struck something suspended from the ceiling and he recoiled, nearly shouting. He immediately shoved Daniel to his knees and pulled his .45 from the holster, both light and weapon pointed at what he had bumped into, a hanging bundle of some kind, about two feet long and twisting slowly from the contact with his head. As it finally reached the nadir of its rotations, it stopped and he got a glimpse of dried and matted fur sticking out of the cocoon before it began to spin back the other way.

"Fuck," he said. "I think you're in a world of trouble right now, padre."

"I think we both are," Daniel whispered.

Chitwood grabbed the pastor roughly by the shoulder again and dragged him to his feet, holstering the .45 and steering Daniel back toward the stairs. He knew the man had killed Jenny, knew she was probably stuffed in that crazy cardboard fort in the corner, and he also knew he was too close to this. If he was the one to find Jenny, he'd most likely beat this tiny fucker to death.

*It depends on how well he can take a punch. And how many it will take to tire me out.*

No. He needed to go by the book from here on out.

But as he pushed Daniel back toward the stairs, a shadow detached itself from the ceiling above him, and he found himself staring into the face of a strangely beautiful woman.

"Nancy!" Daniel shouted as he was torn from Chitwood's grasp, and the sheriff had no time to react to what was going on behind the face of the woman

*she's a spider she's a goddamned gigantic spider*

before her mouth opened impossibly wide and she sunk her needle teeth into his shoulder.

With a howl of pain he shoved her away, his jacket instantly drenched with the blood that was gushing from his shoulder. He pulled his .45 again, but the weapon and his Mag Lite slipped from his fingers and fell to the floor as his arm went cold and numb. He knew he was in real trouble - that bite had torn off a significant portion of his deltoid - but he still had time to wonder, *'Nancy? Isn't that the wife's name?*

The beam from the Mag Lite skittered across the basement floor, finally rolling to a stop and illuminating a horror in the corner Chitwood had missed in the darkness: the body of an old man, his shirt sodden with blood that still looked wet, fresh.

*This is so much more than just Jenny.*

He kneeled, almost fell, scooping up the gun in his left hand. *All the good that'll do.* He was a solid shot with his dominant hand, couldn't hit shit with his left. He staggered to his feet, wanting to somehow put pressure on the wound that was dumping so much blood down his shirt, but he dared not tie up his only free hand.

The streak of ice that was spreading throughout his body from that wound wasn't just shock, he knew that much. Her bite was clearly venomous, and its paralyzing effect was already taking hold.

"Call for help!" he cried out, immediately feeling foolish, realizing just now that Jenny was mistaken about the minister's wife. The Cooks were in on this together, and who knew how many more people they'd murdered in this nightmare basement?

Chitwood backed slowly towards the stairs, his left hand sweeping the gun out in front of him, ready to blast at the first sign of movement in the dark, but he could feel that arm going numb as well.

*You're not making it out of this one, chump.*

His thoughts flashed to the breakup with Jenny, the ugly things he'd said in the heat of the moment and the regret he felt over it; to the time he'd planted coke on a murder suspect so that he could search the man's vehicle; to a physics test he'd been caught cheating on in high school; to a sharp and specific memory of his father assuring him there was nothing under his bed when he'd screamed himself awake after a particularly bad childhood nightmare.

The monster lunged from the darkness again, and it *was* a monster, just like the one in that childhood nightmare, and it had taken fifty years to find him but it *had* found him, and as it dug its teeth into his left arm, he fired the gun.

The report was deafening in the concrete basement, but the bullet was true, striking the creature under its abominably human face and throwing it backwards. It roared in pain and fury, skittering and flopping on its back, and in the peripheral glow from his Mag Lite, Chitwood could see all its limbs slapping and clawing reflexively at the air.

He squeezed the trigger again, the bullet missing and gouging a huge chip out of the concrete floor. His entire body continued to freeze and fail, shutting down on him. The creature screamed and hissed in agony, its many legs still thrashing about.

Chitwood stumbled towards the twitching monster, forcing one foot in front of the other until he was somehow standing above it, revolted, *offended* that this creature was allowed to share space in the universe with the human race.

His .45 was impossibly heavy now, but he mustered the will to raise it slightly and point it at the creature's head. At this range, there would be no missing, and if destroying this abomination was the only good thing he'd ever done, then he'd led a life with a higher purpose.

There was only the briefest moment of shock when he realized the razor-sharp tip of a kitchen knife was protruding from the front of his throat. The paralysis that was affecting the rest of his body spared him most of the pain, but he was choking on his own blood now, unable to even bring his hands to his neck. His vision went dim, and finally black, and the last thing he thought was that after this he needed to go back to Jenny and beg forgiveness, maybe even get his tooth fixed. And then he toppled to the floor next to Nancy, dead.

Daniel stood above him, his hands finally bloody, his eyes wide with madness and shock and horror. He had killed for his wife, but it had been for naught. He dropped to his knees next to Nancy's twitching, hairy body. "Oh, babydoll," he whispered through his tears. "Babydoll."

She smiled up at him at their old nickname, her mouth nightmarish and inhuman, and he positioned himself as well as possible in an attempt to cradle her dying body.

"Daniel…" she said.

He nodded and tried to smile back. "Shh, shh," he said, rocking her gently as the tears ran down his face. She reached up with one twitching, multi-jointed finger to stroke his cheek. Suddenly, her limbs spasmed then slowly curled inward, and although her dull red eyes could not close, Daniel knew she had died.

# 3

Daniel sat with Nancy's strange, dead body cradled in his bloody hands for nearly an hour. He studied her face, and in its alien beauty, he found again much of what he had always been attracted to. Her bizarre fingers looked nearly translucent under the thick, wiry hair that sprouted from every follicle, and there was a beauty in that as well, a utilitarianism, a brilliant efficiency. As he gently stroked those fingers, his skin caught on the wedding ring he'd presented to her twenty-five years earlier, now nearly completely covered by the tough, chitinous skin that had grown over and around it, and he lamented the time he'd spent worrying and stressing over her sickness and subsequent transformation.

All that time had been wasted, lost to him now, and he desperately wished that he had spent it just loving her while she was alive.

When the faint but unmistakable beat in his head began, he thought it must be a sign of impending heart attack or stroke.

It came as a triplet, *bum bum-bum,* and now he could clearly make out the words that accompanied it, although he didn't understand them. The secret language of spiders, he supposed.

*The deputies aren't coming,* he realized. *And you have a job to do.*

Laying Nancy's head gently upon the basement floor, he got to work.

It took Daniel almost two hours to drag Rawlik's corpse up the stairs and into the church proper. The big man's body may have been emptied of all its fluids, but it had been replaced with cargo more precious than his lifeblood.

More precious, and heavier. At the end of the task, Daniel was in agony, his back and knee throbbing in excruciating time with the triplet that was beating through the entirety of his soul, now.

At one point he had neared giving up completely, exhausted beyond words, beyond imagination, but the gentle movement he'd felt stirring within Rawlik's body had re-energized him, and he fought through the pain.

Outside, he brushed away the snow that covered the old, original church marquee and lit it up, surprised that most of the bulbs still worked. The black, oversized plastic letters were stored in the back of the marquee, slightly moldy from years of neglect, but still serviceable. He set to work on his message.

He was startled at the realization he was being observed from the sidewalk, but it was only one of the homeless men who had been so disappointed at the lack of coffee after last week's sermon was cut short.

Daniel smiled at the man and nodded at the message he had created on the sign. "Hope to see you tonight," he said.

The man seemed surprised. "Really?"

"Of course," Daniel said. "And tell your friends. All are welcome."

He turned away from the vagrant, then froze as movement down the street caught his eye.

A dark Toyota Camry had rounded the corner and was heading towards the church, driving slowly even for the icy conditions. It stopped promptly in front of the pastor and his marquee.

Daniel put on his best, most welcoming smile, raising a hand to wave, but when the driver's window rolled down, he felt a cold sweat suddenly break on his forehead.

Deputy Walsh looked back at him from behind the steering wheel, Marlboro dangling from his lower lip.

*I'm sorry Nancy,* Daniel thought, crushed. *I was so close to making it happen.*

But the deputy only glanced at the message on the marquee and smiled, eyes roving from the homeless man to Daniel. He nodded and raised one hand, saluting Daniel with an extended thumb, and Daniel could see that the Camry's back seat was full of books and clothes and a duffel bag and even a nightstand, all hastily and haphazardly jammed together until nothing else could possibly fit.

And then the Camry's window rolled up and Walsh drove off, heading out of Kobbe's End.

Daniel wondered at his fortune, then turned and beamed at the homeless man. "See you tonight." He limped back to the church's entrance, leaving the vagrant to continue his own trek to the tent encampment down the road, where he let everyone know that, according to the church's marquee, there was a "Congregation Appreciation Dinner" this evening, and "all are welcome," and to make it even clearer, the words "Free Food" had been added underneath the announcement.

And there was much rejoicing.

Daniel was astonished at the turnout, but he realized he had greatly underestimated the extent of the humanity that had been packed into all those tents in the vacant lot next to Morgret & Sons.

There must have been over sixty people lined up to enter the tiny church, and it pleased Daniel that most of his regulars had also seen the sign and were interested in the event as well. He had a strange moment of déjà vu as everyone filed in and found places to sit on the old pews, but he brushed it aside, eager to get on with the event.

He shook the hands of anyone who cared for it, including little Kimmy Helman's hand, as she shyly explained (between prompts from her mother) that she was very sorry about last week's incident and would be on her best behavior tonight.

Daniel laughed, latching the big church doors behind them. "Oh, it's nothing to worry about anymore." As they turned and searched for a space to sit, Daniel briskly set the doors' slot locks on the floor and ceiling. Only little Kimmy noticed, as she watched over the shoulder of her mother, but she couldn't have realized what it meant.

He made his way through the crowd towards the lectern, thrilled to see so many people in the audience. This would be the church's biggest attendance since the Cooks had arrived so many years back. Beyond the lectern, he had covered the huge abstract cross statue with an old velvet church curtain, massive and nearly as heavy again as Rawlik's body had been, but Daniel had no worry that the giant steel art piece would support all the weight.

He rapped his knuckles loudly on the lectern's slanted surface until there was silence in the hall, and he gazed out upon his audience with genuine appreciation.

Most of them looked bored, barely willing to sit through his sermon for the promise of free food, and a number of them were actively craning their heads, trying to suss out where all this free food might actually be. But some of them, a very small few of them, seemed genuinely interested in what he had to say, and so he focused on them.

"Hello," he said, warmly. "Hello. Thank you all for coming. I have just a few short words before the feast, if you'll indulge an old widower. As many of you know, my wife, Nancy, has been ill for a very long time. Well... she passed away this morning."

A ripple of general unease spread across the room, and Daniel had to remind himself that none of these people really knew Nancy or him, and he had to concede that most people probably would not have planned a big shindig on the day their wife died. But he was under a bit of a time crunch.

"You know," he said, trying to brush past the discomfort that was permeating the room, "For the last several months of her illness, Nancy had been holding out for a miracle. Long after I had given up, she kept searching for some sign from God that things would turn around. And I think she finally got one. I really believe that. But you know… miracles are messy. They don't often manifest the way we want them to."

His audience had finally quieted, and even the homeless contingent seemed interested. Unsure, but curious where this was leading.

"Believing in miracles is…" he searched for a word, finally found it with a small, sad laugh. "*Complex.* To believe in miracles and have them come true is almost as difficult as believing in them and having them be false, isn't it? I mean, not believing in miracles is a much easier way to go through life."

He smiled, feeling good for the first time in many months about a sermon, especially one being delivered on the fly. "By the eighteen-fifties," he continued, "we had explained most of the Biblical miracles away as simple ignorance. As we better understood the laws of nature, nothing could be called exactly *miraculous* anymore."

The de facto congregation seemed actually interested, not so much because of the particular sermon, he realized, but because it's easy to get caught up in a charismatic man, a man who has faith in his beliefs. And today, Daniel believed. Today, he was absolutely *dripping* with faith.

He continued, "And now here we are in the future, the twenty-first century, and it seems we're starting to really understand how little we *actually* understand, you know? How illogical much of the Universe is… and must continue to be. For the sake of our sanity."

He thumped his fist against the lectern loud enough to startle several people, and he smiled at them, full of love, but ready to get to the main course. "So," he said, "Not so long ago, it was considered 'intelligent' to be suspicious of miracles. We've grown up in an age where miracles simply do not exist. But I wonder now…" He looked out over his audience, finding Lauren Helman, who was absolutely picking up what he was laying down. He grinned at her and almost wished she and Kimmy hadn't come tonight. Not that it would have mattered. "I wonder now if it's time to believe again?"

Daniel stepped away from the lectern and grabbed the old velvet curtain that covered that giant, ridiculous art installation. He gave it a powerful, dramatic yank, pleased with how it unfurled and even more pleased with the collective gasp that it elicited from his congregation.

Strapped to the cross with that old, heavy chain from the basement was the naked body of Peter Rawlik, withered and dead and covered in strange scars and tattoos, his arms tied to the crossbeams in a familiar and surely blasphemous way, all the moisture from his skin very recently sucked dry, leaving a desiccated, almost mummified corpse.

As expected, Daniel's congregation was less than receptive. They rose from their seats almost as one, scrambling for the door in a horrified but surprisingly controlled mass of humanity that had agreed on one thing - a collective "nope" to whatever the fuck was going on here.

The first few of them hit the back doors hard, slamming down on the door bars to no avail, and the second wave of people hit immediately after, piling against them and the doors that refused to budge. No one seemed to notice the locks at the floor and ceiling, and even if they had, the crush of humanity made it impossible for anyone close enough to actually unlatch those locks, and they all began to panic, shouting and screaming in anger and pain.

"Wait!" Daniel commanded loudly from the stage, and the terrified crowd turned back towards him, eyes and mouths stretched wide with fear. He motioned to the dead man he had strapped so meticulously to the oversized cross. "You haven't seen the miracle yet."

The room quieted and seemed to hold its breath, all eyes on Rawlik.

The big man's body spasmed, and the crowd murmured uneasily - had they been mistaken? Was the man, despite his obvious appearance, somehow still alive? As if to feed those doubts, Rawlik's head lurched backwards violently, his jaw working up and down as if in ecstasy.

Daniel saw Lauren in the crush of people by the door, clutching Kimmy's tiny body to her and staring in shock at Rawlik's mouth, unconsciously leaning forward, desperate to hear the words of the dead man…

But it was not secrets that whispered from between Rawlik's cold, dry lips. Instead, one small, slender, chitinous spider leg poked through, followed by the rest of the tiny, hairy monster. It was about the size of a golf ball, all twitching limbs and gnashing teeth… and a miniature face that was abominably human.

It tumbled down the man's nude body, but before it had even reached the carpet beneath him, another fun-sized monster had pried itself out and fallen from Rawlik's mouth, and then, as the trapped humans screamed in terror and revulsion, dozens of the spiderlings spilled forth, and then hundreds, and as they hit the floor, the monsters were instinctively drawn towards the crush of food at the end of the hall.

And now the wails of human fear turned into a roar of terror as bodies were trampled trying to avoid the wave of nestlings that were racing towards them. Daniel watched serenely as Lauren and Kimmy fell to the floor, lost in the rioting crowd, squashed underfoot.

The spider babies overtook the humans, crawling up pant legs and sleeves, cuffs and collars, forcing themselves into mouths and ears and even nostrils, biting the entire time, biting, biting, biting.

And as all those terrified people jittered like fools, screaming and slapping at themselves, Daniel had to laugh. He just couldn't help himself. It was all so funny, so ridiculous. He thought of Nancy and her unshakeable faith. *You always said I'd make a great father.*

He noticed movement on the lectern. Crawling up the side, a hairy, mottled horror of multi-jointed limbs. Daniel smiled at the ghastly human face that was fused to its thorax, and as he went completely, irrevocably mad, one final thought struck him:

*He has my eyes.*

# epilogue:

# Tillman's Depths

Daniel waited for the screaming to die down, and then he made his way past the pleading eyes and frothing mouths to the door that led to the townhouse, unlocking it with the tiny slot key from his pants pocket.

As his children feasted, Daniel went back down to the cellar and collected Nancy. He carried her up the cramped basement stairs, no longer minding the torn muscles in his back or the infection that had spread from his knee throughout his body, or the fever that threatened to consume him from within.

He ferried her strange corpse out of the church and into the freezing night, where he could still hear the occasional moan from a dying churchgoer, and then began his trek through the snowy streets of Kobbe's End for the last time.

He felt the pull of Tillman's Depths working on him like a giant magnet, dragging him irresistibly towards its dark shores, a physical feeling that could not be denied, the triplet beating strong and ferociously through his entire being, now.

*Rho Natus. Rho Natus. Rho Natus.*

The screaming started again as he passed the canvas city, and he turned sharply to realize he was being followed, that hundreds of his spiderlings were trailing behind him, a parade of golf ball-sized killing machines, and he at the head of it like some bizarre, pied piper.

Several spider babies were leaping into the 'End's vacant lot, streaming over and into the tents and lean-tos, supping on the few residents that hadn't taken advantage of the church's offer of free food.

As a heavy wind blew through the surrounding trees, many of the spiderlings let loose webbing that floated on the breeze and then magically dragged their plump little bodies into the sky, to soon deposit them somewhere else, their new homes, perhaps miles away, just as that great spider migration had done one hundred and fifty-some years earlier.

Some of the tiny monsters streamed up concrete walks to the houses that were still occupied, and he heard a few startled - and then agonized - shouts as the spiderlings feasted on the last inhabitants of Kobbe's End, their gossamer already strung from roof to roof and telephone pole to telephone pole.

But most of his children followed him as he slowly carried their mother's corpse past the buildings and the houses, and then down the old logging road, and even as he began slowly wading into the freezing water of moonlit Tillman's Depths, first knee-deep, then quickly chest-deep, the lake water flowing over and then taking hold of Nancy's body as if it knew she belonged there. He clutched her tightly, not bothering to hold his breath as he was pulled completely underwater with her, down, down, down into the darkness of their new home.

# AFTERWORD

What a long, strange journey this has been. This novel began life as a screenplay called *Widowed* back in 2009. It was a much simpler story back then, just a small town minister whose wife was turning into a giant spider. SyFy channel kind of stuff. The script was optioned, and then nothing ever became of it.

In 2017, I revisited it when I was putting together a pitch for a Netflix series about a haunted town called Kobbe's End. The protagonist in that story was a young Hollywood director who had returned to his hometown after his latest cinematic failure. He was accompanied by the ghost of his very dead and very angry Hollywood starlet girlfriend, and together they would unravel the mysterious history of Kobbe's End and its terrifying lake and discover the identity of the serial killer that was terrorizing the small town. See, the new deputy had discovered that the minister's wife was turning into a spider, and he was compelled to sacrifice victims to her. I thought it was a pretty groovy idea for a series, but again I could find no traction with it.

In 2022, I decided to just novelize the damn thing, going back to the original script. It was mostly just to keep myself busy, but the death of a loved one's father lit a fire under my ass to really get it done. I wanted something that I could dedicate to my parents while they were still around. And I did that, making it available as a very limited, illustrated novella.

My editor for the novella (the wonderful Andrea Garland) convinced me there was a much richer story to tell concerning the unfortunate souls that called Kobbe's End home, and she didn't think it was the glossy Netflix pitch I had originally wanted to tell. She thought there was more to be mined in the police that worked in such a tiny town. Or the homeless camp next to the hardware store.

So immediately after releasing the *Widowed* novella, I moved directly into expanding it into a full length novel. Part of that was writing the prequel chapter that became "The Testament of Decraine Kobbe."

I made a VERY limited run of "The Testament of Decraine Kobbe" as an excerpt chapbook. I thought it would make a nice gift for close friends, but one of those friends then casually mentioned that I should release the entire novel in chapbook form. A serialized, monthly novel, which was, of course, absolutely preposterous.

I set out to accomplish it posthaste. I roped in my dear friend Wade Chitwood to illustrate the covers and in 2023 I released this novel in five very limited, monthly installments, complete with holographic, glow-in-the-dark stickers, bookmarks, postcards and photos of the town founders. It sold out immediately, and if you missed that, I am bummed for you. It was really cool, and something I know I will never attempt again.

But even this complete novel version is slightly different from those. I received excellent feedback from amazing cheerleaders in my life who have pointed out a few things I didn't get quite right in the serialized format. I hope I have fixed those story errors satisfactorily for readers of this final edition.

It goes without saying that Kobbe's End doesn't exist, but it is similar in many ways to the town I find myself living in today. To make it a little more bearable, I have populated it with people who share the names of my friends and family. Please know that if I have used your name in this book, whether in service to heroic or villainous acts, it was done with absolute love.

*k!*

*January, 2024*

K.L. Young is an award-winning filmmaker, publisher, and podcaster. He lives in a pop-culture museum in Washington State.

This is his first novel.

Printed in Great Britain
by Amazon